Freeman Wills Crofts was born
died in 1957. He worked for a
company as an engineer until 1929, before turning to detective fiction.

His plots reveal his mathematical training and he specialised in the seemingly unbreakable alibi and the intricacies of railway timetables. He also loved ships and trains and they feature in many of his stories.

Crofts' best-known character is Inspector Joseph French. French appears for the first time in *Inspector French's Greatest Case*. He is a detective who achieves his results through dogged persistence.

Raymond Chandler praised Crofts' plots, calling him 'the soundest builder of them all'.

BY THE SAME AUTHOR
ALL PUBLISHED BY HOUSE OF STRATUS

THE 12.30 FROM CROYDON
THE AFFAIR AT LITTLE WOKEHAM
ANTIDOTE TO VENOM
ANYTHING TO DECLARE?
THE BOX OFFICE MURDERS
THE CASK
CRIME AT GUILDFORD
DEATH OF A TRAIN
DEATH ON THE WAY
THE END OF ANDREW HARRISON
ENEMY UNSEEN
FATAL VENTURE
FEAR COMES TO CHALFONT
FOUND FLOATING
GOLDEN ASHES
THE GROOTE PARK MURDER
THE HOG'S BACK MYSTERY
INSPECTOR FRENCH AND THE CHEYNE MYSTERY
INSPECTOR FRENCH AND THE STARVEL TRAGEDY
INSPECTOR FRENCH'S GREATEST CASE
JAMES TARRANT, ADVENTURER
A LOSING GAME
THE LOSS OF THE JANE VOSPER
MAN OVERBOARD!
MANY A SLIP
MYSTERY IN THE CHANNEL
MURDERERS MAKE MISTAKES
MYSTERY OF THE SLEEPING CAR EXPRESS
MYSTERY ON SOUTHAMPTON WATER
THE PIT-PROP SYNDICATE
THE PONSON CASE
THE SEA MYSTERY
SILENCE FOR THE MURDERER
SIR JOHN MAGILL'S LAST JOURNEY
SUDDEN DEATH

CONTENTS

– 1 –

IN THE NATURE OF A PROLOGUE

Brigadier Rodney Vale, DSO and bar, walked slowly along a footpath which led across the fields of the flat country lying between Radbury on the eastern shore of the Bristol Channel, and the rising ground which culminates in Dunford Hill, some miles inland. He was on his way home after a ten-mile tramp over this high ground, a concession to his belief that such occasional exercise kept him fit. Also he had enjoyed the view thus obtained. He was fond of the sea, but his home, Cheddon House, stood on the low ground a couple of miles inland, so he could see neither the water nor the Welsh coast beyond, as he would have liked. He could smell the estuary, and in thick weather the horns of the steamers creeping up to Cardiff or Avonmouth or Bristol came clearly across the plain, but to see it he had to go to Radbury or climb on to one of the surrounding hills.

It was early September and a perfect morning. Any person free to walk in such pleasant country on such a day should have been happy and contented. Rodney Vale was neither. He was worried about his life and what he should do with it.

He had had a brilliant school and college career, and had then begun to read for the bar with the idea of going into politics, standing for Parliament and eventually getting a place in the Government. Then the war had come. For him it had been an opportunity.

To the abilities he had already shown he now quickly added sound judgment, rapid decision and a willingness to accept responsibility. When invalided out of the Army after four years' service he had obtained his brigade and decoration.

To pick up his civilian life where he laid it down would have seemed his obvious course on his return home. But this he did not appear able to do. Some unsettling of his inner being had taken place and he could no longer concentrate on the dry bones of English law. He had remained at Cheddon House, living in part what used to be called the life of a country gentleman, and in part vanishing for odd days to London, where owing to the money he was able to put in, he had become a director of certain small firms. But none of these activities had been sufficient to absorb his energies. He wanted something with excitement and adventure, and so far he had been unable to find it.

His path led him across the main railway between Bristol and Taunton and over the lands of a neighbouring farmer. This man was ingenious and go-ahead and was always inventing new gadgets. His biggest experiment to date was connected with ensilage, of which he had made a special study. He was constructing a new kind of silo, which he believed would far surpass anything previously thought of. It was to be of the pit type, and close by the path a tremendous hole was being dug. He had explained his idea to Rodney, but beyond the fact that it was in some way connected with bacteria in the lower soil, Rodney had not followed the details.

Standing gazing into the hole was the engineer in charge, a local man whom Rodney knew. Rodney hailed him.

"Morning, Garland. How're things?"

The man turned slowly and smiled. "Morning, Brigadier. Struggling on; struggling on. Looks like going down to Australia with this job."

Rodney stopped and surveyed the activity beneath. "You've certainly scooped out a tidy hole," he admitted. "Have you to take it much deeper?"

" 'Bout another five feet. It's not deep as excavations go, only about thirty feet, but it's big for a silo. Unfortunately it's bad ground, clay and shale with a suspicion of running sand. A bit tricky to build on."

"Will you pile?"

"Not if we can avoid it. Another five feet may get us through the sand."

Rodney nodded and held out his cigarette case. "Interesting work, yours. I saw a bit of earthwork when I was serving in Persia. With both the railway and the oil people."

Garland took a cigarette and brought out his lighter. "I've never been in Persia, but I've been near the frontier from Baghdad. Terrible country, I thought."

They discussed Eastern terrains, then Garland went on: "If you're interested in geology, would you care to see our excavation? Unusual strata, different from anything I've come across before."

"Thanks," said Rodney, "I'd like it. Though I don't know anything about it except as an amateur."

The pit suggested to Rodney a great water butt some thirty feet in diameter by what looked a great deal more than twenty-five feet in depth. It was crisscrossed with heavy struts supporting the timbers with which the upper fifteen feet was close sheeted. Below that was the clay and shale, which would stand safely without support, at least for a time. As they approached, the foreman called out dinner hour and all the men stopped work and climbed out from below.

"Shall I go first?" Garland suggested, beginning to descend one of the ladders leading to the bottom.

Rodney followed and soon stood with the engineer on one of a series of planks which were laid about the floor. The strata were clearly defined and Rodney was interested in examining the layers and dips and comparing them with those he had seen in Persia. For some minutes he chatted with Garland, then he said he must be getting along.

"I expect we'll be beginning the concreting in a week," Garland remarked as they climbed to ground level.

"I'll come and have another look, if I may. Many thanks: I've been interested."

Rodney walked off as slowly as he had approached. But when he was out of sight of the workings his pace quickened and a spring came into his step. His eye had brightened, his expression had become more eager, and all signs of lassitude and dissatisfaction had disappeared.

As he swung along he wondered had he at last found the excitement and adventure he had so long sought.

– 2 –

FAMILY CONCLAVE

On a dark evening exactly a fortnight after Rodney Vale's call at the silo excavation, his cousin by marriage, Pauline Selmer, stepped out of her house, Cheddon Bungalow. Having made sure that her torch and keys were in her bag, she drew the door to after her, shook it to see that it was fastened, and set off with quick steps into the night.

She was not going far, only indeed the three hundred yards which separated her bungalow from Cheddon House, where lived Sir Leigh Vale, his three sons Maurice, Rupert and Rodney and his daughter Anne, respectively uncle and cousins of her husband. Knowing every step of the way she did not use her torch, but strode on without hesitation, guided only by the more inky black of the shrub masses against the sky. A moist breeze from the sea blew in her face across the couple of miles of flat land which lay between Cheddon and the estuary.

Cheddon was an estate and farm, large as estates and farms go today, and her uncle by marriage, Sir Leigh, was the owner. He lived in "The House"; she, wife of George Selmer, nephew and estate agent, occupied "The Bungalow". Both houses were Georgian, solid and dignified and built of grey local stone. Outwardly they remained unaltered, but within both had been drastically modernized and contained all the amenities desired by present-day occupiers.

Pauline had been slightly excited since earlier in the day Rodney had invited her and her husband George to pay the call. Rodney had been excited too. Though he pretended to his usual calm, she could see that he was fighting down strong feeling. Also he had been mysterious. He had pledged them both to silence about the visit. Rodney, though by no means phlegmatic, was not easily excited, and she felt that only some event of major importance could have so moved him.

Pauline got on with her husband's relatives as well as most wives with their in-laws. She had an admiration, almost an affection, for the head of the family, Sir Leigh, though her feelings towards the three sons were curiously mixed. Maurice, the eldest, she liked and respected. He was good and kind and honourable, but a certain distance in his manner made real friendship difficult. Rupert, the next, she could not get on with, though he was always polite to her and indeed was pleasant to all. He was supposed to be the black sheep of the family. Some early scandal, the details of which she had never learned, had necessitated his hurriedly leaving the country. He had gone to America, but had returned on the outbreak of war, and serving with the Eighth Army in North Africa, had there obtained his majority. The fact that he had reached only this rank made the success of his younger brother an embarrassment to both and military matters were seldom mentioned. Anne, the sister, who came next, was a dear, and Pauline's best friend in the family.

Of the youngest, Rodney, Pauline had grown really fond. He was nearer her own age, thirty-two to her thirty. A good fellow in many ways, he was sensible, hard working and extremely competent; kindly also, at least where kindliness did not conflict with his own interests. He had been good to her since her marriage and had stood by her on occasions when she needed help. But she could not hide from herself that he had his defects. Success – or what he called success – was his god. Money, position, power: for these she believed he would have bartered his soul. Where such were in the balance, the interests of others would have small weight.

Since he had been invalided out of the Army she had been unhappy about him. He seemed to have lost interest in his political career and to be somewhat like a fish out of water. Now, walking on through the darkness, she hoped that he had found some interest which would turn his thoughts in a fresh direction and take him out of himself.

At length the considerable bulk of Cheddon House loomed up before her. Lights in the windows and porch showed her the steps leading to the door. She rang.

"Good evening, Lamson," she said when the door opened. "How is Sir Leigh tonight?"

"Pretty well, madam," the butler answered as he took her wraps. "He has had a good day. He's expecting you, madam, if you'll be kind enough to go to the smoking-room."

Sir Leigh Vale was ailing. In his seventieth year, he had till recently been a hale and active man, but now he was losing energy and grip. He still went out on fine days, but his interest in his neighbours and the farm had waned. The doctor, usually an optimist, had not been encouraging about him. He had advised a nurse and an elderly Ulsterwoman had recently been engaged.

Sir Leigh and Rupert were seated before a blazing log fire when Pauline entered. Though slumped forward in his chair, it could still be seen that Sir Leigh had been a fine figure of a man in his day. His face remained striking, with its strong features, deep hollows, dark piercing eyes and mass of white hair. Even now he gave an impression of character and determination. In no throng could he have passed unnoticed. Rupert's features bore a certain resemblance to his father's, but he was smaller and stouter and had a vaguely dissipated look. He rose and pulled forward a chair for Pauline.

Sir Leigh threw down the journal he was reading. "Ah, Pauline, come in," he welcomed her, but without rising. "Are you all alone? I thought George was coming too?"

"George is following on. He wanted to see one of the men about some change in tomorrow's work." Pauline took the chair with a word of thanks to Rupert.

"He's not lazy: I will say that about George. Wonder what Rodney's up to now? Very mysterious and all that about our meeting."

"Some scheme he's keen on," Rupert essayed. "He'll expect us to be keen too."

"He does seem excited about it, whatever it is," said Pauline. "I shall be glad if he's found something to interest him at last. He's really been at a loose end since he left the Army."

Sir Leigh grunted. "Pity he didn't go on with his law. However, he was a sick man when he came home and one couldn't urge him. Not that urging would have made any difference."

"No," Rupert agreed, "Rodney certainly knows his own mind."

Sir Leigh shrugged. "Well," he turned again to Pauline, "what's the news with you? When's George going to London?"

They chatted desultorily till a sudden step was heard in the hall without. "Ah," Sir Leigh remarked, "here's Rodney. Well, Rodney, what's all the fuss about?"

Pauline glanced at the youngest son as he entered the room. She saw a man of medium height and slight build, with small well-shaped hands and feet. His movements were brisk and he still retained his military carriage. He had Sir Leigh's eyes, but the remainder of his features were less spectacular. His expression was sharp: against her will Pauline sometimes thought it foxy. Rodney looked one who could not easily be deceived, but the converse of this was by no means so certain.

"Something I want to talk to you about," he said shortly. "But what about George, Pauline? Isn't he coming?"

"He should be here. He went round to see one of the men. That's he, I expect."

A ring sounded, followed by voices in the hall, and the door opened. The man who entered was tall and broad-shouldered and well set up, though he walked with a slight limp. His features were good, but a close inspection vaguely suggested weakness of character. His expression was bad-tempered and his glance slightly shifty. There were subtle indications of fast living and he was obviously strained and anxious. But his manner was pleasant enough as he greeted Sir Leigh and nodded to Rupert and Rodney.

"I see I'm not the last," he went on. "Didn't you say Maurice was to be here too?"

"Yes, I told him." Rodney's voice was petulant. "Where is he? Do you know, pater?"

Sir Leigh gestured. "Now is it likely that I'd know? Nobody ever tells me anything. Galsworthy knew his stuff all right."

Some moments of rather uneasy conversation followed. Pauline was interested. There was no doubt that Rodney was on edge. His movements were jerky. Twice he lit cigarettes and twice he threw them unsmoked into the fire, significant actions in these times of shortage. Presently he sprang to his feet as if he could no longer endure inaction.

"Maurice said he'd be here," he declared protestingly. "I can't think why he doesn't come. He's not likely to be painting at this hour."

"Might be," suggested Rupert. "He doesn't work to schedule."

"Yes, try his studio," Pauline advised. "He potters about, thinking over what he's going to do next."

"Don't I know it." Rodney vanished, very nearly slamming the door.

"He's wound up all right," went on Pauline. "It's a long time since I've seen him so excited."

They began again to talk about Rodney's future, till presently he re-entered, followed by his brother.

Maurice, like Rupert, was shorter than Rodney, but more stoutly built. He too had Sir Leigh's features, but they were subtly modified. Maurice indeed looked commonplace. Less intelligent than Rodney but a good deal more honest, would have been the average man's diagnosis on seeing them together. There was also a suggestion of rigidity in his make-up, which would be called determination or pigheadedness according to the point of view. It was in fact true that if Maurice once decided on a course of action, it would take something really drastic to turn him from it. But he had many saving graces. He was straight and unselfish and invariably put what he considered his duty before pleasure. A weak heart had precluded military service.

"Forgot about the blessed meeting," he announced as he nodded to the others. "Well, Rodney, what's the trouble, now you've got us here?"

Rodney looked scandalized at this off-hand treatment of a serious subject. However he controlled himself. He waited till Maurice had settled down in a fifth easy-chair, then took up his position on the hearth-rug and glanced round.

As Pauline looked at the two she could not help feeling once again that latent antagonism between them which at times became so obvious. They always seemed to get across one another, and deep down she believed they hated each other. Yet in their way both were good-hearted. Incompatibility of temperament, she supposed, was the operative phrase.

"I asked you to meet like this because something of extraordinary importance has happened," Rodney began. "It may affect very profoundly the lives of all of us; in fact, it must do so. I'm only sorry that Anne's in America and can't discuss it with us. We shall have to take big decisions and there can be no going back on what we do."

Maurice moved impatiently. "Bless us, Rodney, you talk like the chairman at a shareholders' meeting," he observed testily. "What is it that has happened?"

"It's good technique," George pointed out; "what I believe is called preparation."

Rodney scowled at them both, but again controlled himself. "I'll tell you. You may have heard me speak of a chap called Mallow in Persia? He was locating for oil for the British Government: I suppose for the Persians too. In the course of my work I came across him a lot and once when I had leave I spent it with him. None of that of course matters, except to explain how it is that I got to know quite a bit about oil and oil bearing strata, where oil is likely, and all that sort of thing."

He paused. No one commented and he went on. "A fortnight ago I happened to be passing where Arrow is building his silo. Garland Brothers are doing it for him and young Garland was there. I stopped to pass the time of day."

"Decent fellow," said George. "I've seen a lot of him."

"He's a good chap," Rodney agreed. "They've dug a tremendous hole, but except that it's to be a new form of silo, I don't know what they're going to put in it. However that doesn't matter either. Garland asked me was I interested in geology and when I said yes, in an amateurish way, he invited me in to have a look. Well, I suppose by this time you've guessed what I'm coming to. At the bottom of that hole I saw indications which suggested they weren't far from oil."

This at last produced a reaction. "Oil! Good Lord!" Sir Leigh exclaimed, while Rupert sat up sharply. George's eyes flashed and even Maurice looked interested.

"I sounded Garland and satisfied myself that no such idea had occurred to him. Naturally I didn't show undue interest and after a little more chat we parted as casually as we'd met."

"But were you sure oil was there?" asked Sir Leigh.

"No, how could I be? I'm only an amateur. Besides I couldn't make a proper examination. But I was suspicious. It seemed to me there was an oily seepage at the bottom of the pit. But of course I couldn't be sure that oil had not been spilt from one of the machines."

"I thought natural oil would look different," put in George. "What do you say, Rupert? You've seen oil workings in California."

Rupert shrugged. “I’d have thought so, but I wouldn’t know enough to say.”

“Probably you’re both right,” Rodney conceded. “It looked to me to be natural, but I wasn’t certain.”

“What matter whether there was oil there or not?” Maurice interrupted.

Rodney looked at him speculatively. “Well, I thought it might matter quite a bit,” he answered. “I thought at least it was worth trying to find out.”

“What did you do?” Pauline put in, partly to help on the tale and partly because she was really interested.

“I sent for a geological map of the district and saw that Arrow’s ground was on an outcrop. From the dip of the strata I imagined that if there was oil there at all, it would probably be found under this estate and all across the low-lying ground between here and Radbury and over towards Axworth. But of course there again that’s only an amateur’s opinion.”

“So you’re still not sure?” Sir Leigh repeated.

“Let me go on. I felt I must have some further information, so I got it. I went out at two o’clock one morning with a trowel and had a look round. The ladders were still in the pit and I climbed down. I cleaned the bottom and dug some samples from undisturbed soil. I filled a bag with them and managed to get back here unseen.”

Pauline was amazed and she could see that the others shared her feelings. “Rodney!” she exclaimed. “I can’t believe it! You climbing about other people’s property in the night!”

“Why didn’t you tell me about it, Rodney?” George exclaimed. “I’d have given you a hand.”

“Yes, my word!” declared Rupert. “So would I, and glad to.”

"I didn't want to say anything till I had rather more to go on."

"Two can do a job of that sort better than one," George insisted.

"I'll ask you both another time."

"I don't think it was very dignified," Maurice declared.

"Dignified or not dignified, I got the samples. Next day I went to town and employed a confidential agent to send them to Ramsbottom and Clive, the assayers."

"Why did you not send them direct?" Pauline demanded.

"My dear girl, you haven't grasped this," Rodney returned irritably. "Do think for a moment. Well, this morning I got their report through the agent. It was encouraging. They said that oil of good quality was present and probably in quantity, but that without inspecting the site they could not be certain of the amount."

"You've something there," George exclaimed. Pauline could see he was controlling strong excitement.

"I'll say so." She had never seen Rupert so much aroused.

Maurice moved abruptly. "You haven't answered my question."

"I wasn't aware that you had asked one," returned Rodney, and Pauline could almost have wept at the malicious sweetness of his tone.

"I asked what matter it was whether there was oil there or not?"

"Well, that's what I called this meeting to discuss. You must all see – even you, Maurice, must see – that here's a chance of simply fabulous wealth. I say a chance because I don't know yet enough to say more. But there's another thing that you must all see equally, and that is that if a hint of the idea gets about, the chance is lost."

Sir Leigh cleared his throat. "This is very astounding news, Rodney," he pronounced. "Most unexpected. It certainly raises some matters for discussion. What are your own ideas?"

"Well," Rodney answered, "there's really only one question at issue. Are we to take advantage of this chance – supposing it exists – or are we to throw it away?"

"Can there be any such question?" Rupert demanded, perhaps rhetorically, and George nodded his emphatic agreement.

"What would it mean – to take advantage of it?" Pauline asked. She felt slightly overwhelmed by the vista that appeared to be opening out.

"Ah, now you're talking. First, it would mean getting an expert on the job, and we'd have to work out how that was to be done without giving the thing away. There are various ways of testing for oil: gravity, magnetic, electrical, and so on. In one, for example, you drill a hole in the ground and explode a charge at the bottom. The vibrations go down and are reflected up again from various strata, and are picked up on what are called seismic detectors."

"It sounds complicated." Sir Leigh seemed interested, but only academically.

"Yes, it's complicated all right. But of course that method might not be the best to use here. If anything of that sort were done, it would have to be under cover of some other job: we could give out that we were boring an artesian well, for example."

"It could easily be covered," George considered.

This sounded very distasteful to Pauline. However, it must be discussed. "Suppose there is oil?" she suggested.

Maurice made a gesture. "I think I can answer that and without any scientific tests. We would do nothing."

"Nothing?" Rodney's tone was deadly. "You mean you'd throw away the chance of millions?"

"Of course I'd throw away the chance of millions. What do you take me for? I think you've gone out of your mind, Rodney. We've got a bit of nice country here, a bit of England still unspoiled, and you'd dig it all up and destroy it and put up, I suppose, derricks or some other foul contraptions. Cover the Somerset uplands with Midland slums. Not for all the millions in creation!"

"Well," said Sir Leigh judicially, "that's another point of view. There's a good deal in both. We must discuss them thoroughly. What are your further proposals, Rodney?"

Rodney glanced distastefully at his brother. "If it's a true bill I should quietly buy up as much of the surrounding land as we could get. Here again it would be ostensibly for some other job: a housing estate or experimental farm or something of that kind, I don't know now, but we could think up something."

"It could be arranged," George agreed again.

"Yes, of course," Rupert added. "Perfectly easy to fix up something."

Pauline shivered. "Oh, Rodney, I don't like it: all that deceit. Surely it could be done more honestly?"

"I expect it could; I've not gone into it yet. The finding of the oil would have to be kept quiet, because otherwise prices would rocket to the skies. We'd pay perfectly fair prices and do everything quite honourably."

"For the moment you needn't worry about the precise definition of words like 'fair' and 'honourable'." Sir Leigh put in sardonically. "What else do you propose, Rodney?"

"Before we could do anything we'd have to get Anne's views. If the rest of you were favourable I'd fly out and see her. I rather imagine she'd be on for working the oil, but of course I can't be sure."

Pauline thought so too. Anne was more like Rodney than Maurice in disposition and had done equally well in the war, having been Commandant in one of the women's services. She was spending six months with American friends and from her letters was having the time of her life.

"Of course it's understood you'd have to see Anne," Sir Leigh agreed. "But what then?"

"I think in fairness we'd have to let Arrow in. Then I suggest that we'd begin by entering into an agreement that each of us, including Arrow, would help on the project as we were able and in return be allocated a definite share of the profits. The amount each would get would be reached by agreement and if it would help matters I'd propose that our shares be equal."

"You should have more than the others," George put in.

"Yes, of course you should, Rodney," Pauline added. "It would be absurd for me to have the same as you."

"Well, if you feel that way we won't quarrel. I think I should have a little more myself, but I'd take an equal share to get agreement."

"An agreement wouldn't be a difficulty," Rupert considered.

"Aren't you counting your chickens?" Sir Leigh asked testily. "Shouldn't you wait till you knew you had spoils before worrying about their division?"

"That's the first bit of sense we've heard," remarked Maurice, "seeing there won't be any spoils."

"I only meant that anything we might get would be divided among us all," said Rodney, obviously fighting down a more bitter reply.

"All right, Rodney," Sir Leigh closed the discussion. "Profits, if any, are to be divided all round. Any further proposals?"

"When we had the ground I'd suggest handing over to some firm to work the oil on a royalty basis, then clearing out."

"Oh?" cried Pauline, "you don't mean we'd have to give up this house?"

"No need to," Maurice growled. "If you like living in a blastworks with smoke and filth everywhere. For my part I wouldn't condemn a dog to it."

"I'm afraid this house would have to go," Rodney admitted. "But then we'd all have so much money we could build the house of our dreams anywhere in the world."

"Well, I'll have none of it." Maurice got up. "That all you want?"

"No," said Rodney. "Sit down again. There's a lot more."

Maurice sank back into his chair and Rodney continued. "The thing isn't quite so simple as that, Maurice. I, an amateur, tumbled to this possibility through the chance that I'd seen oil working in Persia. But other people, engineers among them, may see that pit, and if so it's even chances that someone else will get the same idea. Or in spite of my care, the fact that I've made inquiries may leak out. Then what happens?"

Rodney paused rhetorically, but no one answering his question, he was forced to do so himself.

"Everything takes place that we've been considering, with one exception. The amenities of the country are spoiled, half the place becomes a slum, we have to leave this house – all just the same. The one thing different is that we don't get the money. We leave beggars instead of millionaires."

"You've certainly got it figured out," Rupert declared. "It's what would happen," while George enthusiastically agreed.

"Carrying on your argument," Sir Leigh observed with detachment, "if the house were taken there'd be compensation."

"No doubt we'd be offered some trifle. If we didn't think it enough, we needn't accept it. Work would go on all round us. They'd know we couldn't stick it very long."

There was silence for a moment, then Rodney went on: "And remember, at the start we wouldn't know what was being hatched. We might find out that land was quietly changing hands, but we might not. In any case it would be too late then. The oil would go to the early bird."

"I shouldn't have thought," put in George, "there was a moment to be lost," and this time it was Rupert who nodded his approval.

Sir Leigh moved jerkily. " 'Pon my soul, George, you and Rodney are harrowing us. This is not a proposition, I may say, that I would normally consider for a moment, but really you're making quite a case for it."

"Trust Rodney to do that," Maurice grumbled. "We've always known he could talk the hind leg off a donkey. But I for one will not be taken in. This place has been in our family for generations and it's up to us to preserve it, even if some of us want to turn it into an inferno."

Pauline could see that both brothers were keeping their tempers with difficulty. She began to fear one of those dreadful outbreaks which had on occasion taken place between them. Rodney was purposely casual as he remarked: "Perhaps Maurice will tell us how he would propose to preserve it if all the surrounding lands were being worked for oil?"

"Aye," said Sir Leigh, apparently also fearing a clash, "that's a point. It's certainly a problem. This thing will take a deal of thinking over."

"If it became known, this place is doomed," George declared firmly. "There's nothing surer than that."

Rodney seemed to have himself once again in hand. "There's another thing to consider," he went on in more normal tones, "and it's perhaps the most important of all. One of the things that this country wants more than any other is home-produced oil. You probably know as well as I do the steps the Government have taken and are taking about it. If we could help to get oil out of this Severn basin, we should be doing more for England, and perhaps the peace of the world, than anything else you could imagine."

"The less we're dependent on the Middle East, the better certainly," Rupert asserted.

"I'm afraid you're both right there," Sir Leigh admitted slowly.

Pauline could feel the despondency in his tone. To most people this news of Rodney's would have been like a glimpse into Paradise. Not so to Sir Leigh. Added to the hatred of change and upset of the infirm and old, he loved the place for its own sake. This solid uncompromising old house was his home, his family seat. Here his forebears had lived, here he himself had been born and brought up, and here he had returned after a life spent in the service of his country. He had hoped to leave it to his sons as his father had left it to him, and the thought that it might vanish from the earth was bitter.

To Pauline also the news had come as a shock. She scarcely knew whether or not she wished the scheme to materialize, so many were the problems it would raise in her life. But the idea of it frightened her.

As she sat listening to the ensuing conversation, somewhat desultory because the minds of all were so full, it was borne in on her that agreement would not be reached. Then she saw that agreement was unnecessary: the matter would automatically settle itself. This was due to the details of the succession, which gave the right of veto to each member of the family.

The estate was entailed. After Sir Leigh it went to Maurice, Rupert, Anne, Rodney and George, in that order, or to their children, if any. With it was included a considerable capital sum which formed a sort of endowment.

From this it followed that the property could only be sold or given another form by consent of all the heirs. In other words, one dissentient could block Rodney's scheme.

Pauline could see that Sir Leigh was growing tired and she had just decided to propose an adjournment when he himself suggested that perhaps they might reach a conclusion.

"I don't know whether you have made up your minds," he said, "but I have made up mine. I feel that this is not a matter for me. I've kept the old place going during my time, but my time is nearly up. You are the people that this proposal would affect and you must settle it. I will agree to anything. Now" – he glanced round – "in all courts martial the youngest member is the first to give his views. It's a good general principle, and I suggest that Pauline lets us hear hers. Technically speaking, of course, she's only interested as George's wife, but I think by this time we all consider her an equal member of the family."

Pauline did not think it such a good principle; however, she warmed to the old man's words. Controlling her feelings, she tried to speak clearly as well as sympathetically to Rodney.

"This thing has come of course as a tremendous surprise, and it's a bit too big for me to sum up on all at once. I'm afraid I've not reached any very definite opinion. There seems to me a tremendous lot to be said on both sides and I think we should consider it further. Rodney has made a strong case: first, the money; then the fact that if we don't get this oil someone else may, in which event we'd have all the drawbacks without any of the advantages; and third, the suggestion that it may be our duty to act for the sake of the country. Every one of these arguments is strong, and the three together are tremendous. On the other hand, as far as feeling and sentiment are concerned, I do agree with Maurice. Maurice hasn't told us all his views, but I do agree about wanting to keep the old family property. Of course it's not a matter for me personally, but you're all so good that I feel as if it was. However, there it is: I honestly don't know what to say."

It was rather a speech, but it seemed to please all of them. Sir Leigh nodded. "I'm not surprised you find it difficult. George is the next, so to speak, junior, in that he is fifth in the entail. Come on, George, let's hear your comments."

George grinned. "I can answer without much hesitation. I should be wholly in favour of acting as Rodney suggests, and without the loss of a day. I think it would be an absolute disaster for all of us if the oil were worked by someone else. And we must all agree with Rodney that only prompt action can ensure that that won't happen."

"Well," Sir Leigh remarked, "that's a straightforward opinion. We're glad to have it. What about you, Rupert?"

Rupert made a decisive gesture. "I'm with Rodney and George all the way. If oil is there, someone will tumble to it sooner or later and everything that Maurice objects to will happen. As we can't prevent this, I don't see why we shouldn't get what we can out of it."

"That's clear enough also." Sir Leigh turned to Rodney. "Your views we know, or do we? Would you like to add anything to what you've said, Rodney?"

"Only that I agree with Rupert and George and that personally I shouldn't hesitate. I've thought the thing over very carefully for several days and I'm quite clear in my own mind. Of course I see Maurice's and Pauline's point about our old family place. I agree with that fully. I agree that this is a choice, if you like, of evils. But I think the arguments for going ahead far outweigh those for sitting tight."

"And I don't agree," Maurice put in without waiting for Sir Leigh's invitation. "You've all been very judicial and I'll try to be the same. I recognize the force of all Rodney's arguments: we all must do so. But I think the arguments against the scheme are stronger still. Here's England, the finest country in the world, and more than half of it has been destroyed by industrialization. So much so, that we're getting short of open country, even short of agricultural land. Here we've got a stretch of country – I don't say it's the most beautiful in the land: it isn't – but it's charming enough in its own way and we can't afford to lose it."

"There's a lot in that view also," Sir Leigh admitted.

"Oil the country can buy abroad. You say, we haven't the money. Well, if not, it's only a temporary shortage and we can do without something else till the pinch is over. But if our open lands go, they're lost forever. I've been speaking from the nation's point of view," Maurice began to grow more heated in spite of himself, "but we must be considered too. I know we come second to the nation, but that doesn't mean we've no standing. Here's our home.

We're fond of it and we're fond of the country round it. It's been ours for hundreds of years and I for one hope it may be ours for hundreds to come."

"The money?" put in Rodney softly.

"The money? We don't want the blasted money. We have enough. Enough to keep the place up, enough to travel, enough to do anything in reason that we wish. What more do we want? What would we do with a million, if we had it? What could we do, except use it to make still more money? Well, I needn't go on talking. I'm sorry, Rodney, but I'm voting against your scheme. I don't see how I could do anything else."

"If someone else opens up?"

"If someone else opens up I'm not responsible. If I open up, I am. I'll take the risk."

From that nothing would move him. He had the power to veto the idea and he was going to use it. No doubt he sincerely believed he was in the right, and who was to say he was not? But Pauline sighed as she saw the glance of concentrated malice, of positive hate, which Rodney gave him. They would be lucky, she thought, if the affair blew over without further trouble.

They had made a move when Rodney halted them. "Just one point. It's understood, I take it, that not one of us breathes a word of any of this: not to anyone on earth? An unintentional leak, and the damage is done."

All agreed to this and all pledged themselves. Five minutes later the party broke up. George went down to his office in the farm buildings to leave some further instructions about the change of work in the morning, and Pauline walked home alone.

– 3 –

FAMILY DISTRESS

Pauline had plenty to think of as she made her way back to the Bungalow. If Rodney's scheme were to materialize it would profoundly affect them all. Maurice of course would fight it tooth and nail, but his opposition might be overcome. Rodney had a habit of getting his own way and he was not always too scrupulous about the means he employed to do it. With a slight shiver it occurred to her that he would be quite capable of giving away the secret himself, provided his own position in any resulting organization were assured. Rupert and George would back the scheme with all their weight and Anne, she thought, would do the same.

She would have been less than human if its effect upon herself did not quickly fill her mind. Pauline's life was not without its problems and one of the chief concerned her husband. After fighting desperately to avoid it, she had been forced to recognize that her marriage had been a mistake. George Selmer was not the man she had imagined. This discovery of oil, if it came to anything, would profoundly affect her relations with him. If he had plenty of money and no job he might go to pieces altogether, which would bring the deterioration in their relations to a head.

Her thoughts ran back over the years. Her earliest recollections were of Cheltenham, where her father, a retired naval commander, had settled down with his three daughters. Pauline never knew her mother, who had died at her birth. When she finished with school she remained idle for a couple of years, undecided as to what to do with her life. Then her father died and the home was broken up. She went out to India to visit some friends and while there the war broke out and civilian travel became difficult. She took up nursing and helped in one of the military hospitals which sprang up near where she was staying. When the war was over it was some time before she could get a berth to return home, with the result that when she reached England it was after an absence of nearly ten years.

The homecoming to which she had been so eagerly looking forward proved a bitter disappointment. She joined her elder sister, who with her husband was living near Axworth. They welcomed her cordially enough, but Pauline soon found that to be a guest, even of her sister's, left a good deal to be desired. Moreover she did not hit it off with Grace's husband. She felt she would soon outstay her welcome. She had enough money to live on, but nothing to claim her interest, and she began to consider taking up nursing as a profession.

Then a new factor came into her life: she met George Selmer.

Selmer was the son of Sir Leigh's younger sister. He was a fine upstanding man, but a wound received in the attack on Narvik had left him with a stiff knee and he had been invalided out of the Navy. During a visit to Cheddon while convalescent he had revealed a considerable knowledge of farming, and as Sir Leigh was becoming too infirm to continue the management of the estate, he offered George the post of agent. George accepted gratefully and moved to the Bungalow, which became recognized as the agent's house. There he was somewhat sketchily looked after by the wife of one of his labourers.

To Pauline, who met him at various social functions, he seemed a pleasant acquaintance. He had travelled and could talk entertainingly on most subjects. The two saw an increasing amount of each other, and Pauline was amused at first and then thrilled when she found that most of the meetings were of his contriving. He was attentive to her, deferring to her opinions and sharing her small interests. In due course the natural result ensued. She fell in love with him and when he asked her to marry him she consented.

For some time after the marriage life for Pauline was sheer bliss. Then gradually doubts began to creep in. After months of growing disillusionment she at last realized that George did not really love her, but had married her to obtain an unpaid housekeeper. He became moody and bad-tempered and disputes between them developed. During one of these it came out that he was gambling on the Stock Exchange. From then she realized that his temper was a barometer of his gains and losses. More than once also she found him, if not drunk, at least fuddled. On one of these occasions they had their first serious quarrel. This had blown over with an apology from George.

But if Pauline's relations with her husband deteriorated, she grew closer to her in-laws. More and more she took to spending time at Cheddon Hall, and though she never breathed a word of her feelings towards George, she felt that these were not unsuspected. It was therefore a great distress to her when, as delicately as he could, Dr Manning informed them that Sir Leigh was suffering from an illness which must shortly prove fatal. He had recommended a nurse and the Ulsterwoman was engaged.

Then it was that Rodney called his meeting about the oil. If oil were worked they would all have to leave the district and break their local ties. As far as she herself was concerned she felt she would not mind if she never saw the place again. Away from Cheddon and its gossip, moreover, it would be easier to separate from George, perhaps even, if he gave her cause, to divorce him. Her lost freedom now seemed very precious to her. She began indeed to hope that the scheme would go on.

When therefore a day or two later Rodney approached her again on the matter, she met him more sympathetically. She now agreed, so she told him, that if there was oil it ought to be worked, and she would no longer oppose the idea on the ground that the old house and estate should be preserved.

Rodney was clearly delighted. "Splendid!" he declared. "That leaves Maurice in a minority of one. We're getting on."

"But are we?" Pauline retorted. "Maurice is like the Russians at UNO, he has the power of veto. And somehow I think he'll use it."

"I dare say we can get to work on Maurice. If once his objection was overcome there'd be no other difficulty, for I'm sure Anne will be all right. Rupert and George are both dead keen."

"Personally I'd like to see the scheme go ahead. But not, Rodney, as long as your father is here. It would worry him though he mightn't say anything."

Rodney nodded. "I agree. But nothing could be done that he need know about. There would be a lot of preliminaries. If Maurice's opposition were to be overcome tomorrow, we should not be ready to start work on the ground for some months, and from what Manning said the pater is not likely to be with us so long."

"I'm afraid you're right."

There was a pause. Then Rodney glanced questioningly at his companion. "There's another point," he went on slowly. "It seems rather callous to speak of it, but we must be practical. When the pater – er – when the end comes, there'll be money available. We – "

Pauline was distressed. "Oh, Rodney, need you talk of that now?"

"Yes, old thing, I must. As I say, it seems callous, but it isn't really. We've got to think ahead. So far as we know, after death duties are paid there'll be about £90,000 from the pater's private money. I've seen the will: it's a strange document. Under it money will be divided between Maurice, Rupert, Anne, George and me: Maurice, Rupert, Anne and I as children will get £20,000 each: George as a nephew £10,000."

"What's strange in that?"

"Nothing: so far it's normal enough. But there's a conditional clause. If any one of us five, Maurice, Rupert, Anne, myself and George, get involved in divorce proceedings up to the time of the grant of probate, we forfeit our legacy. That's not what you'd call normal."

Pauline stared. "It must be unique, I think. Of course your father has tremendously strong views on marriage."

"He thinks all our troubles are due to the increase of divorce. It's an obsession with him. But that's by the way. What I want to ask you is, do you think George would agree to using his share with mine to buy up land? If there's no oil, the land remains, and we could probably sell it again without loss. But if there is oil, even that would give us a fortune."

The idea was new to Pauline. She considered it. "If we did that I suppose there'd be rents?" she asked.

"Of course. My idea would only be to get control, not to displace anyone. If an owner sold, he could remain as tenant till the land was wanted for drilling."

She hesitated. "George would probably want to think over that. Rodney. There's quite a lot to be said on both sides."

"Nonsense. He'll do what you tell him."

"You're optimistic, aren't you? But in any case we shouldn't have that money for some time."

"We could borrow on our expectations." He paused again, then turned to her once more. "Look, Pauline, you have a try at Maurice. He hates me and I could only influence him by putting on pressure. But he thinks a lot of you. He'd listen to what you said at all events."

Pauline felt it was not exactly a matter for her and was not anxious to interfere. However, she promised and next day went up to see Maurice in his studio.

He had thrown three attics into one and opened a large north roof light over the resulting area. Maurice took his painting seriously. All his present efforts were studies for the great picture he hoped some day to produce. He was now working at figures, and a well-built and extremely good-looking woman in classical robes was posing on the dais.

"Morning, Mrs Belcher," Pauline smiled at her. "Hullo, Maurice. I didn't know you were busy. Sorry to interrupt."

Maurice stepped back from his easel and stared at his work with half-closed eyes and head on one side. Then he put down his brushes. “Just finished. I’m fed up, Mrs Belcher, so let’s call it a day.”

Mrs Belcher got up and stretched luxuriously. She was tall and statuesque and had a presence.

“You’re not as fed up as I am,” she declared. She moved round and looked at the canvas. “I don’t claim to be good-looking,” she announced in a slow lazy drawl, “but I’m not quite such a fright as you’ve made me, Mr Vale. I look as if I’d a pain in my tummy. What do you think, Mrs Selmer?”

Pauline thought it a moment for diplomacy. “It’s a good pose,” she pronounced critically. “What are you supposed to be looking at?”

“The Emperor,” put in Maurice. “The procession to the Colosseum is passing. She’s looking down from a window and he looks up and sees her.”

“If it’s all like that it’ll be pretty effective.” For some moments they discussed the projected picture and then Mrs Belcher disappeared into a dressing room, a space cut off from a corner of the studio. Pauline changed the subject. “Look here, Maurice, I wanted a word with you about this business of Rodney’s: the oil, you know.”

Maurice’s brow darkened. “Oh that? I can’t see that there’s anything more to be said about it.”

“Rodney’s terribly keen about it and so are Rupert and George. And on the whole I’ve come to agree with them. What about it, Maurice? Do you think you could see your way to join with us?”

Maurice moved uneasily. “My dear Pauline, you’ve heard my reasons. You admitted yourself they were strong. Nothing has occurred to alter any of them.”

“I admit that, but the reasons on the other side are strong too. Will you not think it over?”

He hesitated. "I hate to be disobliging: I really do. But I think I'm standing for what's right. I think the preservation of England is more important than anything else. To me it's a duty."

From this position Pauline could not move him and she left feeling that she had done the scheme harm rather than good. Anxious and troubled as to what might be coming, she returned home without seeing Rodney.

Her feeling of foreboding grew weightier as the days passed. This was due to the general atmosphere of the two houses rather than to any particular incident. Relations between Maurice and Rodney were becoming increasingly strained. Maurice showed little feeling, merely tending to ignore Rodney, but at times the hate in Rodney's eyes terrified Pauline. She grew more and more afraid that some small event might precipitate a disaster. Sir Leigh's influence had kept the peace in the past, but this was declining as the old man grew weaker. Rupert's dry and rather sarcastic remarks, she feared, tended to increase rather than diminish the tension.

Conditions at the Bungalow were no happier. There a new factor had come into the situation which alternately pleased and distressed Pauline. When George came home late in the evening he usually smelt of whisky, but on two or three occasions she fancied she could also detect the odour of perfume. She was not sure and said nothing about it. Then an episode occurred which brought the matter to a head.

One day George left early, saying that he was lunching with some business acquaintances in Radbury and would not be home till dinner. She found during the morning that she wanted a length of some special material to complete the covering of a chair at which she was working. The matter was of no importance, but she was alone all day and at a loose end and she decided to go into Bristol and get the stuff. She had not enough petrol to take her small car all the way, so she drove to Radbury, parked there, and went on by bus.

She duly completed her purchase, lunched, and was returning to the bus, when outside a small hotel in a secluded street she saw a car of the colour and make of George's. It was a common enough model and she did not give the matter a thought until, when she was within fifty feet of the door, George himself emerged. He did not look in her direction, being wholly engrossed in ushering a companion to the car. Pauline's instinct was to step forward and greet him, but when she saw that the companion was a lady of somewhat spectacular appearance, she wished only that the pavement would open and swallow her. Actually she moved behind a red postal box which conveniently stood on the edge of the footpath. But she need not have troubled to hide. George was too much occupied to look round. Having held the door and arranged a rug to the lady's satisfaction, he hurried round to the driver's side, jumped in, and they drove off. But not before Pauline had seen his expression. It gave everything away.

She scarcely knew how she reached home. Conscious only of a numb pain, she felt that this really was the end. She could make no plans, but instinctively concentrated on trying to be normal, so as to gain time and leave herself free to take any action she might later approve.

As the days passed she was surprised to find her reaction to the affair changing, till at last she began to wonder if this was not what she had really wanted. Might she not here have grounds for a divorce? She had by this time realized that her greatest desire in life was to be rid of George.

She was surprised that she had heard nothing more of the oil affair and once or twice she asked Rodney how things were going. He had no news for her. Maurice's attitude was blocking action and he had not yet worked out a plan to overcome his objection. But suddenly the matter was brought once again to the fore and in a very strange and unexpected way.

Pauline was at work with her sewing machine one morning when Rodney called to see her. He was looking both worried and puzzled.

"Well, Rodney," she greeted him. "Come to my workroom: we haven't lit the lounge fire yet." She cleared segments of a garment from an easy-chair. "You seem a bit upset. It's not your father?"

He sat down. "No, no, the pater's all right."

"Something's happened. What is it?"

He looked at her appraisingly. "You're very observant, Pauline. I shouldn't like to have to keep a secret from you."

She laughed. "You couldn't if you didn't do better than that. Why, it stands out a mile. You've obviously come to tell me, so get on with it."

"Matter of fact, you're right," he admitted gravely. "I've had a rather worrying letter." He took an envelope from his pocket. "It came this morning and I don't know what to make of it. Read that."

The letter was typed on a sheet of poor quality paper torn off a cheap block, in accordance, had Pauline realized it, with the best standards of detective fiction. It was headed "Radbury" with the date and read:

Brigadier Rodney Vale, DSO

SIR,

As an admirer of your War record and therefore of yourself, I think it only right to inform you that your maid, Molly Crawford, is spreading a story about you.

She is saying that you have discovered a secret about Radbury which will bring you and your family a fortune. She does not claim to know what the secret is, but has wagered that she will find out.

If there is any truth in her story, it is only fair that you should be warned.

A FELLOW RESIDENT.

Pauline stared stupidly at the document. "But, Rodney," she exclaimed, "it isn't possible! Molly couldn't know. Besides, even if she did, she wouldn't talk like that about it."

Rodney shook his head. "I thought so at first, but now I'm not so sure. She could know. She could have listened at the keyhole to our meeting."

"Oh, but Molly! She wouldn't do it."

"It's the last thing I should have expected, I admit. But it's possible. You say she wouldn't have done it: how do you know?"

"No more than you do, I suppose. I've not had much to do with her. I've always found her competent and sufficiently polite, but certainly close. She's never mentioned her family or anything about herself. How long has she been with you?"

"Couple of years, I should think."

"Well, that should be long enough to establish her character. I don't believe she did anything of the kind."

Rodney made a decisive gesture. "But she did. She must have. The letter proves it. Eavesdropping is the only way she could have learnt."

"But did she learn? Need the letter be true?"

"Of course it must. Look, whoever wrote the letter had heard of the secret. How? If it was not through Molly, it was through you or me or the pater or Rupert or George. Did you go about spreading the story?"

"Don't be silly."

"Well, there you are. I certainly didn't and the pater couldn't have. So if it wasn't Molly it must have been Rupert or George. Is that likely?"

"Again don't be silly."

"After me, Rupert and George were the keenest on the scheme. They would know that without secrecy there could be no profits. Wild horses wouldn't drag information from either. Only Molly is left."

Pauline thought this over. "It seems a true bill," she said slowly. "But I never would have suspected it. What will you do?"

"Dismiss her today."

This seemed rather drastic to Pauline. "Oh but, Rodney, you can't do that. You'd have to prove your charge or you'd have an action for wrongful dismissal: at all events trouble of some kind."

"I've thought of that. I'll make no accusation. I'll tell her that I've no fault to find with her, but that the post is wanted for a friend in financial difficulties. I'll give her three months' wages as compensation and she can have a good testimonial. Actually there's nothing against her work."

"All that isn't true."

"It's sufficiently true. It's the easiest way out: in fact, it's the only way."

"One point occurs to me. Won't the fact that you have dismissed her prove there's something in the story?"

"That's certainly a nasty one. But I can't help it. I must counter the danger of her learning more."

For some time they continued discussing the affair and gradually Pauline became convinced that Rodney's plan was the only one possible. He took his leave and afterwards Pauline learned that an indignant and apparently mystified Molly had taken the afternoon train to Bath, where lived her family.

The very next day the vacancy was filled. Lamson arranged the matter, though how, Pauline did not hear. The new maid, Susan Stewart, was quiet and respectful and seemed competent, but Pauline did not greatly take to her personally.

For some days she could see that Rodney continued on edge. He frequented the better-class Radbury bars, listening avidly for rumours about oil. But he heard none. Apparently no harm had been done and the acute anxiety passed out of his manner.

Rupert had seemed equally upset. "Incredible affair," he declared to Pauline. "Makes you almost believe in telepathy. Rodney did the right thing getting rid of that girl. But I don't think we need worry. If rumours were going round we'd have heard them before this."

Then occurred an episode small in itself, but which surprised Pauline in that for a moment it looked as if it might lead to a reconciliation with George. On two or three recent occasions he had had slight but unpleasant attacks, apparently digestive upsets. These had quickly passed over, leaving no obvious ill results. They had surprised Pauline, for constitutionally George was as strong as a horse and rarely suffered from minor ailments. She had not thought it necessary to call in the doctor.

Now he had another, a considerably worse one. He came home early looking distressed and frightened and saying he felt ill. He could eat no dinner and later was violently sick. Pale and trembling, of his own free will he took the unprecedented step of going early to bed.

Pauline suggested ringing up Dr Manning, but he objected, that it was not necessary. He explained, as she knew, that he had lunched that day in Bristol and felt sure he had eaten something which had disagreed with him. He declared he would be better presently.

She was not fully satisfied, and when nine came and there was no improvement, she did ring up the doctor. Manning came and examined him carefully. He said that from the symptoms he did not think there was anything to worry about, but if George was not better in the morning she should let him know and he would make a further examination.

George seemed to her really ill and it was when she was looking down at him, seemingly weak and helpless, that a faint glimmering of her old love for him returned. He had been lying with his eyes closed, but now he opened them and murmured, “You're good to me, Pauline. I don’t deserve it.”

This she took as an attempt to make amends and decided to meet him halfway. “You did deserve it,” she told him. “Why not deserve it again?”

“You’re a good sort,” he answered. “I know I’ve been drinking and bad tempered. I’ve been worried about money. But I’ve cut out gambling and things should soon be better.”

“I’m glad to hear that.” She hesitated, decided to try an experiment, and then went on: “But, George, since we're discussing it we may as well include everything. It sounds melodramatic, but when you’ve come home I’ve smelled perfume on your clothes and I found a blonde hair on your coat.”

He stared as if perplexed, then his face cleared. “My dear, there’s nothing in that; absolutely nothing whatever, I assure you. That was Mrs Dunstan. As you know, I've been seeing a lot of Dunstan about those new fittings for the byre. There's been trouble in getting just what we wanted. We've been going round the country recently looking at things they'd supplied, and Mrs D and her sister who's staying with them often came for the drive. I have sat, sometimes with one and sometimes with the other, and no doubt traces of scent and hairs have been on my clothes, but there's never been anything between us. My dear, you do believe that?"

She remembered Bristol. Even now he was lying to her. So reconciliation was impossible. She drew back and he sighed, turned over, and reclosed his eyes.

The crisis of the attack seemed to come about ten and from then a slow improvement set in. But it was nearly one before she felt she could go to bed.

"I don't think I need sit up any longer," she told him. "You seem better."

"I am better," he agreed; "I think the attack's over. There's just one thing, Pauline. I'd love a cup of tea. And you could do with one too. What about it?"

"A good idea. I'll make it."

She went to the kitchen and got ready the tea and brought it along. "I've cut some bread and butter," she went on. "Can you manage it?"

"I think so," he answered. "But I'll tell you; if you don't mind, I'd dearly like some of those plain biscuits in the box in the dining-room."

"I'll get them."

They had their tea and she got into bed. She woke later than usual feeling tired and unrested, the result no doubt of the evening's upset. George, who was usually down before her, was still in bed, but opened his eyes as she stirred.

"Oh, better," he said in reply to her question. "All right, in fact. Only I'm dog lazy: don't want to move a finger."

"Better stay in bed for breakfast."

"Not I. I've given trouble enough. I'm all right really and I'll be ready directly."

He did dress quickly though he was not all right. He drank some coffee, but ate practically no breakfast. Pauline was worried about him and wondered whether she should not call in Dr Manning again. She was beginning to discuss it with George when an event happened which put his indisposition and her own misgivings completely out of her mind.

The telephone rang. It was Rodney and his voice frightened her. "Pauline," he said, "I'm afraid I've some bad news for you: really serious."

"Your father?" she returned quickly.

"No, no, not the pater. It's – Maurice."

A great fear seized her. "Maurice?" she breathed. "What's happened?"

"He's met with an accident: terrible, I hate to tell you, but he's been run over on the railway."

Pauline could not believe her ears. "Oh, Rodney! He's not...he's not...dead?"

Rodney's voice had softened. "I'm afraid so. It was instantaneous. He felt nothing."

Pauline's head was swimming. Maurice dead! Killed on the railway. How could such a thing have happened? It was beyond belief.

But Rodney's voice was going on. "Better come up," it said. "You can hear all the details, and I'm sure the pater would like to see you."

"Of course I'll go at once. And George too. He hasn't gone out yet."

She replaced the receiver. George had overheard the conversation and was staring at her. "My God, Pauline, this doesn't mean that Maurice is dead?" he asked in an awestruck voice.

"Dead," she returned numbly. "Run over on the railway. Oh, George, isn't it *awful*! What can have happened?"

"My God!" George repeated. "The railway! Of all places! What could he have been doing there? Come up to the House, Pauline. We must hear more."

"I'm ready," she answered as if in a dream. "I'll go as I am."

George had put the question which was clamouring in her own mind. What had Maurice been doing on the railway? It was fantastic. Yet the mention of the railway had to some extent relieved that wild burst of panic which had swept over her on hearing the news. She was now ashamed of herself, but her instant thought had been of Rodney and whether his hate might not have overswept its barriers. The railway settled that. Rodney could not have had anything to do with the railway. Bitterly she condemned herself for her disloyalty.

The House already had an atmosphere of tragedy. Lamson, pale and distressed, was hovering in a lost way in the hall. He came forward. "Mr Rodney's in the morning room, madam," he said, and there was sympathy in his manner. "He wanted to see you when you came."

"Oh, Lamson, I can't believe it." The old man after all was a friend of the family. "When did you hear?"

"Just a few minutes ago, madam. The sergeant came with the news."

"And Sir Leigh?"

"The nurse said he had borne the shock well."

"Where did it – er – take place?" George asked in a low tone.

"At the level crossing on the footpath to Rockton." As he spoke the door of the morning room opened and Rodney appeared. He was looking deeply distressed. "Come in, Pauline," he invited. "Come in, both of you." He closed the door behind them. "Terrible, isn't it?"

"Oh, Rodney, it's absolutely ghastly. And incredible. Tell us about it."

Rodney pulled chairs forward. "We may as well sit down. It's all you say, ghastly and incredible."

"We just couldn't believe it at first," George declared. "And we couldn't imagine what might have happened."

"I'll tell you. Maurice didn't come down to breakfast this morning and I sent Lamson up. He reported he couldn't find him and his bed had not been slept in."

"Good Lord," said George. "Then he went out last night?"

"He went out all right, or at least he said he was going. Yesterday morning he asked me to go with him to a film in Axworth: something with Persian scenery in it that he thought I'd like. If he'd known how I loathed the country he wouldn't have suggested it. But I took what he said kindly: you know, our relations haven't been too happy since that question of the oil came up. I didn't go, but we chatted about it and parted better friends than for some time."

This still further relieved Pauline's mind. "I'm glad of that," she murmured.

"I'm more glad of it now than I can say," Rodney returned, and there was no mistaking the sincerity in his voice. "But I desperately blame myself for not going with him. I should have done it for the sake of peace. If I had, the accident might not have happened."

"But how did he get to the railway?" asked George. "All right. Sorry. Tell it your own way."

"I don't know how he got to the railway; can't imagine. Well, to go on. We were a bit upset by what Lamson said, because Maurice was always so careful to carry out his plans and to let other people know if he deviated from routine. I began to wonder if we should make a search, but we hadn't decided anything when Sergeant Dutton called. He told us what had happened."

"Let's have the details," George said.

"Of course. He said the railway ganger, inspecting the line before starting work, had found the body at the level crossing on the Rockton footpath. He ran to the nearest telephone and rang up the police. They went out with an ambulance and took the body to their mortuary. The sergeant was sent out with the news."

"Oh, Rodney, it's all just dreadful!" Pauline felt almost sick. "And there's no understanding it."

"Incredible certainly," George agreed. "Had the police any theory?"

"If they had, they didn't mention it."

"He must have felt like a walk, perhaps taken a round from Axworth," Pauline suggested.

"It's not like him," Rodney objected. "All the same that idea is supported by two things. He hadn't taken out his car, and over that crossing is a possible though indirect route from Axworth."

"That must be it."

"But must it?" George demanded. "If he was going to Axworth, why *didn't* he take out his car? It's quite a walk; both ways, I mean."

Rodney shrugged. "I don't know. I wondered about that too."

"Rupert will be distressed," went on Pauline. "Where is he?"

"Didn't you know?" Rodney answered. "He's in London. He went up yesterday morning to the El Alamein reunion. That was last night. I suppose we should send him a wire, but I don't know where he was staying."

"Try the Coniston: I've heard him speak of going there."

"I'll get through on the telephone."

Pauline shivered. "*Poor* Maurice! I can't realize that we've lost him. He had his little peculiarities, but underneath he was pure gold." She paused, then went on: "And then think of all that's going to happen, the police, the publicity." She rose. "Look here, Rodney, I'd like to go up and see your father. It must have been a terrible shock to him."

"I intended to ask you to go. The nurse is there, but I know he'd like to see you."

Nurse M'Candless met Pauline at the invalid's door. "It's given him a knock, Mrs Selmer," she whispered. "Don't talk to him. He'll be glad you're there, but he's better not disturbed."

Sir Leigh indeed looked very frail. He was lying with his eyes closed, but opened them when Pauline approached. "Terrible! Terrible!" he muttered and closed them again. He remained quite still and she thought he was unconscious of her presence. After a little she slipped away and rejoined the others.

"The inquest is bound to be soon," George was saying, "probably tomorrow. But it's not likely to take long."

"No," Rodney agreed. "At the same time these things can be very troublesome. I wonder who they'll want."

"You, and perhaps Lamson. None of the rest of us know anything about it."

"My Lord, but it's a puzzle! The whole thing just doesn't make sense."

"I know," George nodded. "It's all unlike Maurice. It's unlike him to go out in the evening without a word and particularly without telling Lamson when he'd be back. It's unlike him to walk a distance like that when his car was available. It's unlike him..."

Pauline heard them as if in a dream. She felt stunned and incapable of thinking out pros and cons and possibilities. Maurice was gone. That was the one thing that mattered. Though she had nothing with which exactly to reproach herself, she thought she might have been more friendly and helpful to him. But now it was too late.

– 4 –

AN UNHAPPY ACCIDENT

On the afternoon following the death of Maurice Vale Superintendent Joseph French threw down the file of papers he was consulting and leant back in his chair. He was sick to death of these hooligan youngsters with their guns and their coshes and their attacks on defenceless old women. They made his work duller and more sordid than ever, yet the thought of all these young people going wrong distressed him intensely. He did not wholly blame them. The war, housing, careless parents, and the general lowering of moral tone had something to do with it. No doubt there were other causes as well. But whatever these might be, there was the result and quite often he had to deal with it. A *filthy* job!

French was tired and dispirited. It was, he thought, that nasty bout of flu from which he had just recovered – if he had recovered. He didn't seem able to shake off the dregs. One day he would feel reasonably well, the next as bad as ever. And it certainly affected his outlook. Never could he remember feeling so depressed.

He picked up the file. Here was a case in point. What sort of conclusion could one come to about this young John Smith, this sixteen-year-old gangster, who had gone to a lonely cottage to ask for a drink and when the woman had turned to get it had bashed in her skull and ransacked the house? What had made him do it? What poison had worked in his mind…

French's house telephone rang. With a muttered curse at a fresh interruption he lifted the receiver and barked, "Well?"

It was his chief's private secretary. Sir Mortimer Ellison, the Assistant Commissioner, would like to see him if he were disengaged.

French considered with grim amusement the idea of replying that he was busy at the moment, but would go later. In two minutes he was knocking at the AC's door.

"As the sparks fly upward," murmured Sir Mortimer, vaguely indicating a chair. "Sit down, French, it's for you."

"Trouble, sir? I'll survive it."

The AC looked at him speculatively. "Now why do you say that?" he asked with apparent interest. "A bit optimistic surely?"

French knew his chief. His joking way of talking was sometimes hard to live up to, but personally he was of the best: kindly, straight as a die, and absolutely on the top of his job.

"I'm hardened to trouble. Rarely out of it."

"Ah, true. Our common heritage. Well, this time it's down in Somerset. Nice district on the shore of the Bristol Channel. My old friend Major Harwood unearthed it, didn't like it, and unloaded it on me. But I knew something worth two of that. I thought of you before he had well begun."

"You wish me to go down, sir?"

The AC dropped his whimsical manner. "Well, yes, I do," he answered. "It looks like being a big case and I think we should do it proud. This Vale, the man who was killed, comes of a rather important family; big bugs locally. Not of course that that, et cetera. There's the usual difficulty that their CID expert can't act: this time because he's ill. And so he may be for all I know to the contrary."

"Do you wish me to stay on the job, sir?"

The question had some significance. It was not customary for a man in French's position to do more than pay occasional visits to outside cases. This indeed had been one of the drawbacks of promotion. French had always enjoyed working in the country.

"I'm going to give you your choice. Pleasure or dignity. You can either stay down there and act as if in a lower grade, or you can put someone else in charge and go and see him at intervals. As a matter of fact, I thought you might like the change. I imagined you hadn't quite got over your 'flu."

How like the AC! Thoughtful and kind. French did not hesitate. "That's extraordinarily good of you, sir. There's nothing I'd like better than to get into the country for a few days. I'll take Carter, if I may, and it will be like old times."

"I don't know that taking Carter will illuminate the darkness. However, that's up to you. Now the really important thing is settled. As to the man's death, I don't know a thing about it except that you're to call as soon as possible at the police station at Radbury and they'll give you the facts, if any."

The mere prospect of a change subtly improved French's health, and handing the juvenile delinquency file to a subordinate almost completed the cure. A strenuous half-hour of preparation enabled him to catch with Carter the six-thirty from Paddington, and some four hours later they alighted in the charming little western town. Sergeant Dutton was waiting on the platform and a few minutes later they were introducing themselves to Superintendent Bowman at the police station.

"Good of you to come so promptly," Bowman greeted them, for politeness' sake chatting awhile on impersonal subjects. Then he went on: "Well, here's eleven o'clock and I take it, Mr French, you've had enough for one day. We've reserved rooms for you at the Esplanade Hotel, and if you care to go there at once, the sergeant will take you round. Our CC, Major Harwood, will be here at eight-thirty in the morning, and, I think he'd like to tell you about the case himself."

The hotel was comfortable and French felt that apart from the case he was going to enjoy his break from town. Next morning they returned betimes to the police station and had scarcely reassembled in Superintendent Bowman's room when a voice was heard below. "That's the Major," Bowman announced. "He's a friend of the bereaved family and that makes him jumpy about the affair. You'll see."

As he spoke a thickset man with a military bearing and a strong intelligent face entered the room.

"Superintendent French?" he said, holding out his hand. "Glad to see you. And you," he nodded to Carter. Once again they chatted while taking their places round the table, then the CC looked quizzically at French.

"Aren't we rather honoured?" he asked. "I scarcely expected to find an officer of your standing."

French grinned. He would have liked to answer in Sir Mortimer's own vein, but rather doubted Harwood's appreciation. "It was Sir Mortimer's kindness, sir. I've just had 'flu and he gave me a change out of the office."

"Oh," the Major returned without enthusiasm. "A rest cure?"

French thought it better that this should be a joke and he smiled again. "No such luck, sir, I'm afraid. I'm really quite fit again. It was just the chance of a change."

"Oh well, it's OK by me, in the foul phrase. Now, Super, have you told Mr French about the case?"

"No, sir. He's just arrived."

"Very well, I'll tell him and you put me right if necessary. Let's see." The CC picked up some notes. "At seven-fifty yesterday morning the local railway ganger rang up to say he had found the body of a man on the line some mile or more on the Bristol side of Hatton. You, Dutton, got the ambulance and a couple of men and went out."

"Yes, sir."

"Fortunately you had the wit to take a camera and you got some photographs before the body was moved. Here they are."

Some excellent but ghastly enlargements showed that the remains had been badly cut up. The face in particular was almost entirely destroyed and one foot had been severed.

"It was at the side of a pedestrian level crossing, as if the man had been passing over when the train struck him and carried him along. You can see the crossing in one of those pictures."

"I see it, sir; yes."

"Dutton then sent the remains in by the ambulance, while he and one of his men had a look round the place. Just tell Mr French what you found."

"The crossing," explained the sergeant, "is for foot passengers only and is on a path connecting several houses, including the deceased's, on the west side of the line, to a road on the east. It's not much used and the surface is mostly hard, either grass or stone. So it doesn't take footprints. We had a look along it and found only two, both on a patch of sand thrown out by a rabbit. They were on the same side as the deceased's house and were pointing towards the railway."

"Had these prints been made by the shoes on the body?" French asked.

"Yes, sir."

"I see. What else?"

"That's all, sir. We searched round carefully, but couldn't find any other traces."

"By this time the body had come in," resumed the CC. "The face was unrecognizable, but you, Super, went through the pockets and found papers identifying it as that of Mr Maurice Vale, the eldest son of an important landowner, Sir Leigh Vale."

"Yes, sir," Bowman answered. "There were letters and an engagement book and in a wallet an identity card. And in the side pocket of the overcoat were two gloves."

Bowman pronounced this last sentence with an emphasis which made French look up questioningly. "Two gloves?" he repeated.

"Yes, Mr French, two gloves. Soft brown leather gloves rather similar in appearance: a gentleman's left and a lady's right."

This was new in French's experience. He turned to Major Harwood. "A bit suggestive that, sir?"

"Very," the CC returned dryly, "but scarcely in the way you mean. Maurice Vale was an artist, oils: an amateur but pretty good. Thought a lot of in artistic circles and has had pictures hung. He used different models and the lady's glove belongs to one of them, a Mrs Belcher. We've been into that. The man's glove was his own, the butler identified it. Mrs Belcher had recently been sitting for him, and as the gloves are rather alike, he could easily have picked up one of hers by mistake."

French nodded diplomatically, though privately reserving judgment. "That certainly seems to meet the case."

"Yes, completely. I knew the poor fellow well. Friend of the family and all that. Meticulous sort of chap was Maurice. I wonder how many people carry their identity cards these days."

"What age, sir?"

"About forty. Though he has worked hard at his painting, he didn't have to: they've heaps of money. Dutton had the nice job of going out and telling the family. I'd have gone myself, but I was at the other end of the county. That covers everything, I think, Super, till we come to Manning's statement?"

"Yes, that was next."

"Dr Manning examined the body and told us very much what we expected to hear. Death occurred from the injuries received, and he estimated about four hours before he saw the remains. That would be around four in the morning or later. This is borne out by the railway evidence. We had the engines examined and one bore traces of the accident. It worked a goods train which passed the place at four-twenty yesterday morning."

"Pretty conclusive."

"Yes, there's no doubt about that part of it. But now comes something that's not so conclusive, in fact, Mr French," he smiled slightly, "I'm afraid your opinion of me won't bear expression. You will see that the question arises, what was Vale doing out there at four in the morning?"

"Naturally, sir. Have you formed any opinion?"

"Bowman immediately reached that which may have crossed your own mind: the influence of the glove, no doubt. He suggested that Vale had been visiting a lady."

"It would be a natural explanation," French considered.

Harwood made a gesture. "Now that's where you're wrong, if I may say so. It would be so unnatural that I for one could not accept it. The difference between us is that I knew the man. He was old for his age: old in mind, I mean, and his habits were unusually settled. You could foretell what he'd do in any given circumstances, and most of what he'd say. Now just consider. First of all he was not interested in women: I understand there had been some early affair in which he had been rather hard hit. His art absorbed all his energies. Next, he hated going out in the evening and never did so except when he couldn't help himself. When he did go out, he invariably said that he was going and when he'd be back. Now two nights ago he slipped secretly out of the house. He told no one, and no one knew he had gone till the next morning. Then it was found that his bed had not been slept in. So presumably he went out late in the evening. But he was alive till twenty past four. Where was he during the small hours?"

"Does not that rather support the Superintendent's suggestion?"

"Of course it does, and when the facts become known at the inquest that's what everyone will believe. But from my knowledge of the man I don't believe it. So I start with a suspicion that the facts are not quite what they seem."

"Is there anything else to support that opinion, sir?"

"A very proper question, Mr French, which I immediately asked myself. Yes, there is, and it's this. Vale always had his wits about him: I mean, he didn't daydream and become lost to his surroundings. The line at the place of the accident is a four-track one, dead straight in both directions. Trains can be seen and heard approaching from far away. On a calm night a train makes quite a roar and its headlights are clear. Now I can't believe that Vale could have stepped on to the track when one was coming."

"A second train," French suggested. "That's the way people usually are killed on railways. Their attention is taken up avoiding one train and they don't notice the other."

"That's what Bowman suggested, but it doesn't apply in this case, for the deceased had not crossed any lines: the body was on the outside line on the side of the approaching footsteps. No matter what might have been passing further away from him, he would undoubtedly have looked along that first track before stepping on to it."

"It's certainly a point," French admitted.

"I said the suggestion of gloves was scarcely what you assumed," went on Harwood. "It doesn't seem to me a very likely thing that gloves would get mixed up in that way: I mean, of course, by accident. I've tried to work out how it could happen and I haven't found it easy."

"You think, sir, they may have been planted?"

"Put it like this." Major Harwood paused as if he found his explanation difficult. "The doubt is cumulative: first, the man's character, second, his apparent deafness and blindness, and third, the mixing of the gloves. Any one of them means little, any two even are not impressive, but all three together make you think."

They made French think. He thought that Harwood had a bee in his bonnet and that what he wanted was something which would let the family down easily. "What then is your view?" he asked.

Harwood shrugged. "I have none except that I believe there is more in the affair than has come out."

"Is that a suggestion of foul play?"

"No: it's a demand for certainty. You find out what happened, Mr French. We must hope it was an accident, which of course would end the matter."

French was not impressed, but he thought it well to be tactful. "Well, sir, that's clear enough so far as I'm concerned. And since I'm to work on the case I'd like to say how much I appreciate your promptness. Our work is usually doubled by arriving after the scent is cold."

"I'm afraid I scarcely deserve that. Our CID Inspector is on sick leave. The Super has plenty to keep him busy and we have no one else for it. So we'll now hand over to you and I needn't say that all our resources are at your disposal. Just ask Mr Bowman for what you want."

"Thank you very much, sir."

"Just one other word. This is a painful affair for me, because of my friendship with the family. I suppose I was wrong in that: a policeman shouldn't get too intimate with the people in his district; however, there it is. You'll have to ask them questions and so on. Now I don't want you to deviate a hair's breadth from your duty, but I should take it as a favour if you'd make it as easy for the family as that duty allows."

"I understand, sir. You may depend on me."

"Thank you. Then I'll be off."

"He suspects foul play," French remarked when he and Bowman were alone. "I wonder if he knows more than he said? He might think it unfair to mention a name."

"If you ask me, he knows no more than you do yourself." The Super paused, glanced at French, and went on in a lower tone. "You're going to work here, Mr French, and you should know what's whispered. There's a daughter as well as the three sons – Miss Anne Vale. She's from home now and has been for some weeks. It's commonly reported that she's the draw: that the Major wants to marry her. Of course no one knows for sure. But if it's true it would account for his attitude. He'll not want any slur on the deceased's character, and he'll want the family handled easily."

"My word, yes! It's hard lines in his position."

"Yes, awkward for him. Now, Mr French, what would you like to do? Sergeant Dutton will be at your disposal as long as you want him."

"Thank you, then I'd like to begin with the level crossing."

"Good. Take the Morris, Dutton. You can have that car for your own use while you're here, Mr French."

"I can see you're going to do us proud, Super."

After a short drive and walk they reached the railway. It stretched across the plain from north-east to south-west, level and straight in both directions as far as the eye could reach, a great highway connecting the north and east through Bristol with the extreme west through Taunton. As Major Harwood had said, it had here four tracks, the middle two close together, the outer on each side separated from the others by a rather wider space. The crossing was an obvious right of way, with wicket gates at each side and the customary cautionary notices. A gravel path about three feet wide was carried across the tracks at rail level, and French noted that there were no guardrails or timbers inside the rails to keep a clear channel for the wheel flanges. Accidents, he knew, had occurred through people catching their heels in such and being unable to release them in time. It was evident that this had not happened to Maurice

Vale. The path, confined between hedges, stretched away from the wicket gates on either side.

"Where did you find the prints, Sergeant?" French asked.

Dutton led the way along the path on the sea side of the line. Some hundred feet from the crossing was the patch of sand and on it were two very clear prints.

"Good enough," French commented. "Have you taken casts?"

"No, sir; I didn't think it necessary."

"We'd better have them. Start in, Carter, while we're looking round. Any more prints?"

"I didn't go more than a hundred yards further and I didn't see any."

It was evident then that the deceased had walked down to the railway. But he had not been killed till 4.20 a.m. What could have brought him to the place at that hour? If the prints had been on the other side of the line, pointing towards Cheddon, it would have been clear enough: he would then have been returning from his nocturnal escapade. But the marks as they were didn't make sense.

Then an obvious explanation occurred to him. He turned to Dutton. "Where does this lady, this Mrs Belcher, live?"

"Near Rockton, sir, not far from where the path joins the road."

"On the other side of the line?"

"Yes, sir."

"Did you look there for prints?"

An understanding look appeared in the sergeant's eyes. "No, sir, there just wasn't time yesterday. I mentioned it to the Super, but I couldn't get away to do it."

For a moment French unworthily wondered if the CC had prevented the search, then he dismissed the idea as absurd. "We'll have a squint now," he decided.

They crossed the railway and continued along the path. Then satisfaction filled French's mind. On a patch of yellow clay which seemed to outcrop there were two prints. They were both Maurice's, they were pointing in opposite directions, and that facing towards the railway was superimposed on the other.

"A good start," French commented. "We'll have a cast here too." He shouted to Carter. "Carry on, Dutton."

In the short distance to the road they found three other prints, two heading forward and one back. The road of course was hard and bore no traces. French suggested a visit to Mrs Belcher.

She occupied a tiny detached bungalow standing in some quarter of an acre of ground. Want of paint and a somewhat overgrown garden gave it a dilapidated appearance. This, together with the fact that the lady had sat as a model, suggested to French a shortage of cash.

"Is there a Mr Belcher?" he asked.

"Captain Belcher, sir. Master of a merchant ship. Very fine man, but seldom at home."

"Any family or dependants?"

"None but Mrs Belcher, sir. She lives alone."

"Well, keep your eyes skinned as we go to the door."

They passed up the short path and rang. There was no reply. It presently became clear that the lady was from home.

"All the better," said French. "Have a look round. Steady," he went on after a moment, "what's that?"

On a flower bed at the side of the path was a print of Maurice's, perfectly clear, and pointing along the wall towards a window. There were no traces on the grass, but on another bed at the window were several prints. Maurice had evidently stood here for some time, for the ground was trampled, both feet showing close together and pointing inwards. On still another bed approaching the back door were two more prints, indicating that he had walked from the window to the door.

"Better photo those," French decided.

He was pleased with his progress. There could no longer be any doubt as to what had taken place. Maurice Vale had slipped out of his home in the late evening and had walked across the railway to this woman's house. In the early morning he had left, and it was on his return journey that he had been run over. The times now fitted in perfectly.

Something else fitted also. When the man reached the track on which he was killed he was not beginning to cross the line. He had already passed over three other tracks. Therefore the argument of the second train applied. Almost certainly he had been avoiding some other train when the goods caught him. It looked as if French's job was done. He would see the body and check over the various statements, and if everything worked in he would make out his report accordingly. Alas for his change of air to the sea!

They picked up Carter and his casts and drove back to Radbury. There French examined the body, but without learning much that was new. He satisfied himself that the shoes really had made the prints and noted that while they bore traces of mud and what looked like loam, they were cleaner than he would have expected. Then he reminded himself that there was a great difference between walkers. Two people cross the same patch of muddy ground and the shoes of one will be filthy and those of the other practically clean. Maurice must have been a careful walker.

French turned next to the clothes. Maurice had been wearing a brown tweed overcoat and this was marked from contact with the ground. It was possible to distinguish between the markings. Those on the chest and side were dark with traces of oil and rust, obviously from the stone ballast of the railway. But on the back there was what looked like garden mould, the same apparently as the loam on the shoes. It suggested that Maurice had fallen on his back on the path across the railway and been rolled over on to his chest when the engine struck him. All the same, the mould wasn't like the soil of the path, and French put samples from coat and shoes into envelopes, so that the matter might be checked.

The articles in the pockets told French little. The letters had no apparent bearing on the tragedy, nor was there any suggestive entry in the engagement book. The only interesting item was an electric torch, which seemed to stress the deliberate nature of the expedition.

As a matter of routine French went on to see Dr Manning. The doctor simply repeated what the CC had said. Death had been caused by the injuries received from the engine, as these were inflicted when the man was alive, and they would have been immediately fatal. The time of death also worked in. The head, face and neck were badly injured, the face indeed being quite unrecognizable, but there was no doubt that the remains were Maurice Vale's, because of a birth mark on the upper arm which the doctor had noticed when attending him for a slight skin trouble. This had cleared up in due course and at the time of his death Maurice was in a perfectly healthy condition.

"Well, Carter," French said as they left the house, "any objection to an early lunch?"

Carter grinned, as in duty bound. It was a standing joke of French's that his sergeant was only happy when eating, and Carter had found it politic to play up. As a matter of fact, he *was* fond of his food, and why not? So, he told himself, was French. On this occasion both men were hungry and the next half-hour passed pleasantly.

"Now let's go and see these blessed people at Cheddon," French went on when again duty called. "While they're finishing lunch we'll have a look round and get the lie of the land. I don't think we'll want Dutton any more."

The Cheddon House drive left the road from Radbury to Hatton some distance short of the latter. It wound between fields of fine pasture land, and through a copse which screened the House. Round the building was a grass sward with flower beds near the windows and banks of shrubs beyond. A tennis court and greenhouses showed at a little distance, while at the back was a large old-fashioned yard in which the coach houses had been turned into garages. All was tidy and well kept and no lack of money was anywhere apparent.

Before reaching the house the drive divided and the second spur led first to the Bungalow and then on to the farmyard. From the latter a lane gave a separate connection to the road. There was also a footpath running more directly between the dwelling-houses. This formed the continuation of the fatal path across the railway.

By the time all this had been absorbed French thought the family should have finished lunch. He and Carter therefore went to the House and asked for Brigadier Vale.

Rodney saw them in his own sanctum. "Major Harwood was here this morning and told us you'd be coming," he greeted them. "I confess I was surprised when I heard that Scotland Yard had been called in. The Major said he had no reason to think the tragedy was other than a pure accident, but if he's right, why are you here? Or is that an indiscreet question?"

"Not at all, sir, it's a natural one. But I just arrived this morning and you can scarcely expect me to have reached a conclusion so soon. All the same I may say that everything I have seen so far points to accident. It was in the hope that you would help me by answering some questions that I have called."

"Of course I'll help you in any way I can. Ask your questions by all means."

"Thank you, sir. Then not to take up more of your time than is necessary, perhaps you'll tell me about your family?"

Rodney did so. Beginning with his ancestor who had obtained Cheddon several hundred years earlier, he briefly sketched the family fortunes, ending up with the mention of those members still alive.

"Now your brother, Brigadier?"

Rodney told of Maurice's upbringing, his love of art, of the studio he had built, and the studies he was making for his great picture. In reply to further questions he gave similar but more condensed information about himself, Rupert, Pauline and George, and mentioned the various members of the staff.

"Thank you, that's very helpful. Gives me the picture. Now when did you last see your brother?"

"At dinner the night before last. He and I and my father's nurse, Nurse M'Candless, dined together: my father hasn't been well enough recently to come down. After dinner the nurse went off on her business and Maurice and I sat for a while reading in the lounge. Then Maurice said he wanted to look at something in his studio and left the room. I never saw him again. He didn't come down to breakfast yesterday morning, so I sent Lamson up to remind him of the time. He was not there and his bed had not been slept in."

"Was it usual for him to go to his studio in the evening?"

"I don't know that it was usual, but he did it frequently. It did not surprise me."

"Can you say about what time he left you?"

Rodney hesitated. "We dined at seven-thirty and went into the lounge for coffee about eight. I should think about eight-thirty, but I couldn't be certain."

"You didn't hear him go out?"

"No. I heard nothing."

"Can you form any opinion as to what might have taken him out?"

"He said something to me about that, but I don't know if it was his real reason," and Rodney went on to tell of Maurice's invitation to join him at the cinema.

"Since he didn't leave you till eight-thirty, could he have seen the film?"

"If he had taken his car and the picture had been late on the programme I think he could. But he didn't take his car, so I don't know what to say."

French nodded. All this seemed to be working in. If Maurice had wished to pay a secret call on Mrs Belcher, he would be likely to put up some hare of this kind. French grew more confidential.

"Now, sir, I should like to ask some questions which may sound offensive. They are not intended to be so and you will see they are necessary when I ask them. Did you know, or had you any reason to suspect, that Mr Vale might have been interested in some woman?"

Rodney made an almost angry gesture. "I was expecting that question, Mr French, and of course I see what's in your mind. It's that matter of the gloves, isn't it?"

"You must admit, sir, it's the obvious suggestion. It was made at the station, but the Major was very positive that nothing of the kind had taken place. Of course if it were true it would explain the affair. I'm sure you'll agree that the point should be settled."

"Naturally, because if it's not disposed of, it's what everyone will assume. All I can say is that I never had the slightest suspicion of anything of the kind, and knowing Maurice as I did, I find it impossible to believe."

"What about the owner of the glove, Mrs Belcher?"

"Absurd. She's a nice woman, not at all the kind who would lend herself to anything of the sort."

"That's convincing enough. There was a hint that there had been some unhappy love affair in the deceased's life?"

Rodney hesitated. "It's not a thing I know much about or wish to speak of, but I suppose you wouldn't have asked unless it was material. Some years ago Maurice fell rather deeply in love with a certain lady. The wedding day had been fixed when she suddenly jilted him and went off with another man. He showed little sign outwardly, but it was obvious that he was wounded. Since then he avoided women as much as he could."

"Thank you, sir, for answering that. Now can you tell me whether your brother had an enemy? Anyone who might wish to blacken his character by starting a story of an improper visit during the night?"

"No indeed, Mr French, I don't believe he had. He was kindly and inoffensive. Too retiring perhaps to be exactly popular, but he was certainly liked."

"Was he in his usual frame of mind on that last day?"

Rodney paused at this. "I thought he seemed a little worried, but it may have been my imagination."

"Your elder brother, Major Rupert Vale? I understand he's away from home?"

"He was away from home. He went up to the El Alamein reunion. I phoned his hotel and he came back last night."

"And you can't tell me anything else that might help me?"

"I'm afraid not."

Rodney's statement had not been very illuminating, though French thought it all tended towards the conclusion he had already provisionally reached. He was indeed more interested in Rodney's manner than in his story. He was obviously uneasy and French wondered why. Many people became nervous while being interviewed by the police, but a brigadier with Rodney's war record was not likely to be one of them. French could not but wonder if he knew more than he had told.

Naturally he was careful not to betray his interest, merely asking if he could see Rupert. The Major's statement confirmed Rodney's. He had gone to town on the Monday morning and attended the reunion that evening. After the formal meeting he had gone to the Golden Lizard night club till about four in the morning. Later that day Rodney had telephoned and he had come home by the first train. French went on to see Sir Leigh, but neither from him nor Nurse M'Candless did he learn anything new.

Lamson, whom he interviewed next, stated that about eight-thirty on the evening in question he had noticed Maurice leave the lounge and go upstairs as if to his studio. He had not seen him again. Next morning about half-way through breakfast Rodney had rung for him and sent him up to remind Maurice of the time. Maurice's room was empty and his bed had not been slept in. He had searched the studio and other rooms in case Maurice had been taken ill, but there was no sign of him. When Lamson came down he saw that his hat and coat were missing. So far as he knew, Maurice had had no telegrams, telephone calls, or visitors during the day, but he had had four letters by the morning post, all with typed addresses. He had imagined that Maurice had seemed slightly worried that day, but of this he could not be sure.

"Now, Lamson, I suppose you heard that only one of Mr Vale's gloves was found on the body?"

The old man looked distressed. "Yes, sir, Sergeant Dutton showed it to me yesterday and asked me could I identify it."

"And could you?"

"Yes, it was Mr Maurice's."

"He must have dropped the other somewhere. I'm anxious to find it. Could you have a look?"

"I've already done so, sir: the sergeant asked me to. I hunted everywhere, but I couldn't find it."

French was interested to note that these last four witnesses, Rupert, Sir Leigh, the nurse and butler, betrayed no uneasiness whatever. This seemed somehow to bring Rodney's manner into stronger prominence. He thought he had now learnt all that Cheddon House was likely to reveal, and after thanking Lamson, he and Carter took their leave.

– 5 –

A HINT OF MURDER

It was getting on to four as French and Carter drove away from Cheddon House. French had still to see Mrs Belcher, which should finish what he called his field work. He would then only have to complete his report and for him the case would be at an end.

"All seems pretty clear, sir," Carter observed tentatively as they turned east.

It was unusual for the sergeant to express an uninvited opinion and French guessed what had prompted the remark.

"Want to get home, do you? Tomorrow, in all probability. Unless this Mrs Belcher starts some new hare we'll be finished when we've seen her. I'll do my report tonight, we'll unload it on the CC in the morning and catch a midday train."

"Suits me, sir. Tomorrow's my youngest's birthday and the old lady's having a spread for her."

"You'll be pleased and I'll be sorry. I was looking forward to a change at the sea."

"Sea!" returned Carter scornfully, "We might be a hundred miles from it here. I've only had a squint at it from the hotel, and it's not what I'd call sea."

"It's only an estuary," French grinned. "You mustn't blame it. It can't help the way it's made."

As he spoke Mrs Belcher's bungalow came in sight. This time the lady was at home. French was impressed by her appearance, a tall well-built woman with dark hair and eyes, strong clear-cut features and an admirable carriage. She looked straightforward, kindly and efficient, as well as bearing that indescribable stamp of what used to be called good breeding. French knew life too well to be led astray by appearances; at the same time he found it hard to believe that a woman of this type should be party to what he suspected. He raised his hat.

"Good afternoon, madam. Superintendent French and Sergeant Carter of Scotland Yard."

She had looked anxious and worried when she opened the door, but now an expression of positive fear passed over her face. For a moment she remained motionless, evidently fighting it down. Then she stood back from the door. "Won't you come in? I heard in the town this morning that you were here and I expected you'd call. It's about the glove, I suppose?"

They followed her into the small lounge, comfortably if rather cheaply furnished, but spotlessly clean and tidy. It had the pleasant look of being used. She motioned them to chairs.

"I do want to ask your help, Mrs Belcher," French began, "about the glove among other things. You knew it had been found?"

She seemed surprised. "Oh yes, Sergeant Dutton was here yesterday and told me. It's a complete mystery to me. I can't account for it at all."

"I understand you were helping Mr Vale with a picture?"

She smiled a little tremulously. "That's a rather polite way to put it. I sat for him as a model."

"You liked him?"

"Oh yes, he was kind and thoughtful. He paid well and considered my convenience as well as his own."

"A good testimonial, madam. He liked you?"

She sat for some seconds without speaking and he could see her hands clasped till the knuckles showed white. "I think you needn't beat about the bush like that, Mr French. I can see what you're coming to." Her voice grew bitter. "It's been hinted to me already by different busybodies. You think that there was something between us and that Mr Vale was coming here when he was killed?"

"Not exactly, madam. We think he had been here and was killed on his way home."

She jerked back as if from a blow in the face. "But it's not true," she cried, still obviously fighting for calm. "There was nothing whatever between us except the business of the picture. He has never at any time been inside the house. I'm not on the telephone, and if he wanted me to sit for him he'd send a note by the gardener, who lives near. He never came himself."

French was puzzled. His instinct was to believe the woman. On the other hand there were the footprints.

"Madam," he said quietly, "it's not a crime. You must know that that sort of thing is not altogether uncommon. The police are not interested in you or in whether it did or did not take place. All we want is an explanation of Mr Vale's using the level crossing."

"Well, I can't give it. I can only assure you that he didn't come here."

"Were you in the house yourself that night?"

"Yes."

"Alone?"

"Yes, alone."

"Come to the hall door a moment, please. What window is that?"

"My bedroom."

"I thought so. Now, Mrs Belcher, our information is that on the night of his death Mr Vale walked from Cheddon House to that window, that he stood there for some little time and then walked to the back door, that he then walked away from the back door to the level crossing, and that it was then he was killed."

She shook her head distractedly. "Oh no, no, he didn't! It's not true! He never came here!"

"Come out on to the grass." French led the way to the window. "Look there. They're Mr Vale's footprints."

She stared with every appearance of incredulity. "I couldn't have believed it!" she exclaimed at last. "I can't explain it! I never saw him! If he knocked, I never heard him. I never let him in. I never knew he was here. What does it mean, Superintendent?"

French shrugged. "There's the evidence: make what you like of it. Come in again, please. Now," he went on when they were seated, "about the glove. The glove found in his pocket was yours?"

"The glove Sergeant Dutton showed me was mine. He said it was found in his pocket."

"Can you account for its being there?"

"No, absolutely not. I can scarcely even now believe it."

"Did you wear those gloves when you went to Cheddon House?"

"No, I'm sure I did not. They were my best gloves. I only wore them on special occasions."

This still further puzzled French. He wondered had she missed the implication of what she was saying. "Where did you keep them, madam?"

"In a drawer in my room."

"Did you look there since this happened?"

Her face grew ghastly. She seemed unable to reply, then at length whispered, "Yes."

"What did you find?"

She stared at him, then suddenly lowered her head into her hands and burst into a flood of tears. He watched her, feeling acutely uncomfortable. He could not see why she was so upset. As he had told her, no criminal charge was in question. "Madam," he said not unkindly, "please pull yourself together. This is an unpleasant business for us as well as for you, and the sooner it's over the better for us all. What did you find?"

"I found," she whispered hoarsely, "both gloves!"

"Both? You mean that the one in his pocket wasn't yours after all?"

She shook her head. "I found – the other two of the pairs: his and mine!"

This certainly was not what French had expected to hear. "You found Mr Vale's other glove in the drawer in your room? That's surprising. Did you tell that to Sergeant Dutton?"

"No. I didn't look till after he had gone."

French was more puzzled than ever. Surely, he thought, she must know that these admissions were making nonsense of her previous denials? Then the suggestion that the gloves had been planted recurred to him. All this looked not unlike it.

"Tell me, Mrs Belcher, who has a key to your house?"

"I have one and Mrs Rudkin another. That's the wife of the Cheddon gardener who comes twice a week to clean for me."

"Anyone else?"

"No one."

"You're sure Mr Vale hadn't one?"

"Absolutely certain, Superintendent."

French stood up. "Very well, Mrs Belcher, we've had your statement, and if you don't want to add anything to it, that will be all." He paused and she shook her head. "Then I regret this unpleasant interview and wish you good afternoon."

French was silent as they started up the car. Then he turned to Carter. "Well, Sergeant, what do you think of that?"

Carter's opinions, when he could be prevailed upon to express them, were uninspired but often sound enough. "I just don't know, sir. If that was a tale she did it pretty well. All the same, what else could it have been?"

Though not remarkable for clarity, the question summed up French's own ideas. His instincts told him that the woman was speaking the truth, his reason that she was lying. He felt slightly unhappy as he decided that in a conflict between the two, reason must inevitably prevail.

When they reached the station they found that Superintendent Bowman had gone out. They therefore went on to the hotel and French settled down to his report.

With the single exception of Mrs Belcher's personality and manner, the case was clear beyond possibility of doubt. Maurice Vale had slipped secretly out of his house on the night of his death, a proceeding completely at variance with his normal behaviour. The action was deliberate and showed that he was engaged in something of which he did not wish others to know. His footprints demonstrated that he had walked from Cheddon House to Mrs Belcher's bungalow. There he had stood at her window, and what could that have been for save to discuss his entrance? True, there was no proof that the back door had been opened, but why should he have left the window and gone there if it had not been? In any case the point was immaterial. It was when he was returning that he was killed, probably due to the passage of a second train. The medical evidence showed that the accident was genuine: that death had been due to the train and to no other cause. The episode of the gloves was less clear, but there was an obvious explanation which need have no sinister meaning. In spite of her recollection, Mrs Belcher had worn the gloves when visiting Cheddon House. Through a strange coincidence she had put them down near a somewhat similar pair of Maurice's. She had in error picked up one of each when leaving and on reaching home had put them in her drawer. Also not noticing what he was doing, Maurice had picked up the other two and put them in his pocket. As to the possibility of their having been planted, this was ruled out by a simple but convincing consideration. Who could have planted them? And why? No one was in a position to do it and no one had any motive. No one indeed had any reason for faking anything. French martialled his arguments and set them out in what he considered was an excellent report. By the time he had finished it was nearly midnight, and with a grunt of satisfaction over good work well done he went up to bed.

But not to sleep. Some demon of unrest had entered into his being and he tossed, restless and annoyed. Then inevitably his mind turned once more to his case. In spite of the completely satisfying conclusion to which his reason had led him, his instincts obstinately refused to fall into line. He fought against the feeling, but at length he had to admit himself not wholly at ease about the affair.

Sleep being beyond hope, he concentrated on the disquieting points. First, there was a good deal of opinion against his theory. Major Harwood's estimate of Maurice's character absolutely precluded it. Both Major and Brigadier Vale had been equally emphatic. Of course these were a friend and the brothers respectively of the deceased, but that was no reason to doubt their good faith. All were shrewd men of the world whose opinion could not be ignored. Brigadier Vale moreover had spoken in a similar strain about Mrs Belcher.

But much more strongly weighed with French his own opinion of Mrs Belcher. If he were any judge of character the woman was honest. Certain of her admissions recurred to him, and he now thought he had scarcely appreciated their significance. She had admitted that the glove in Maurice's pocket was hers, when, had she denied it, probably no living soul could have proved her wrong. She had told of the finding of Maurice's other glove in her bedroom drawer, when, had she burned the gloves and said nothing, this impressive evidence would have been destroyed.

Why this gratuitous information? Why volunteer what could only injure herself? French at last found himself forced to the conclusion that the lady had made the assertions because they were true. Her native honesty had precluded any other course.

But if so, what about her other statement, insisted on with equal determination? If Maurice had indeed visited her, would her native honesty have allowed her to deny it so convincingly? Then French saw that the fact of the footprints was here decisive. If Maurice had been at her house, Mrs Belcher's appearance of honesty was a fraudulent façade.

Another point worried French: the loam or garden mould on Maurice's back and shoes. He began to wonder whether it really could have come from the path across the rails, as he remembered that this was of yellow clay beaten down to a hard surface. Even if the coat had there obtained its soil, he now saw that by no possibility could the shoes have done so.

He tossed restlessly. It was not the first time he had become dissatisfied with a previously accepted conclusion, and in every such case further investigation had justified his doubts. Irritably he swore at the check. With these doubtful items he dare not leave the matter as it was. Further inquiries would have to be made. On reaching this conclusion sleep came to him, and when he woke his depression had passed away and he was his normal cheery self.

"One or two more points to look into before we go, Carter," he observed at breakfast. "Thought of them in the night."

"Does that mean we'll not be going back today?"

"We will if I can manage it, but I'm not too sure. First thing, I want to go back to that crossing."

They set off in the car, but as they were passing Hatton Station French stopped. Having introduced himself to the stationmaster, he went on: "I'm anxious to know whether a second train could have confused Mr Vale when the goods knocked him down. Any way of finding out?"

"I can tell you at once," the stationmaster answered. "We've only to look up the signalman's block book which gives the times every train was in the section. I wondered myself if that had been the cause of the accident and I looked it up out of curiosity. No other train passed within ten minutes of the goods."

So Major Harwood's point that Maurice would have heard the train was valid. French felt his holding back of the report was already justified.

Presently they reached the crossing. There was no fine dust on it, due, he imagined, to the wind caused by passing trains. But there was yellow clay and of this he took a sample. Nowhere was there anything like garden mould.

Maurice had therefore lain on the ground before reaching the crossing. Surely he had not done so voluntarily. Had he tripped over something in the dark, he would have fallen on his chest. Certainly it was beginning to look as if the CC had been right and that there was more in the affair than had been supposed. French was still more thankful that he had held back the report.

"Look, Carter," he said, "here's the position. The deceased had garden mould on his back and shoes. He didn't get it on the crossing as I had supposed; it's yellow clay there. He was therefore lying on his back on cultivated ground. We've got to find the place."

"My word, sir, that changes the outlook. Maybe the CC wasn't talking through his hat after all."

"Your language, Carter, is a disgrace to the Force. CCs don't talk through their hats, only sergeants do that. Now let's see. We presume that Maurice left Cheddon House and walked here. How would he come? No doubt by that direct footpath. We'll begin with that. We'll walk to the House, you looking out that side and I this."

They moved off, scrutinizing the path surface and edges. "Scarcely likely we'll find any more prints," French remarked when they had passed the two on the patch of sand. Then he pointed. "What's that?"

"Another one right enough," Carter declared. "There can't be much traffic along here or it would have gone."

"The grass tells us that," French pointed out, "and there," he went on when they had walked some fifty yards further, "is another. What work's going on here, I wonder?"

"Some new kind of silo, sir. Dutton happened to mention it."

Just beyond the pit the hedge alongside the path gave place to an iron railing. It bounded a clump of ornamental shrubs, planted apparently to screen the path from the dwelling-house of the farm. The ground beneath these had recently been hoed and was clear of weeds. Suddenly French whistled. Between two shrubs was a print.

Carter was impressed. "Bless us, sir, what was he doing there?"

French grunted. "Lying on his back, I expect. It's the kind of soil at all events. Let's have a squint."

Traces there were in plenty, but all but the one print invisible from the path. Among the shrubs were several more prints of the correct size, though not clear enough to identify with certainty. At one place the soil was flattened down as if it had borne some heavy object, and from the shape of the impression French was sure it was a human body. It seemed certain that Maurice had lain here before he had reached the crossing. But what had brought him to the place French could not imagine.

"Get some pictures," he directed.

While Carter photographed the traces French took a sample of the soil. Then they resumed their walk to Cheddon House. Presently they came to the point they had reached on the previous day. Here the path divided into three, one continuing to the House, the others leading to the Bungalow and farmyard respectively. From here the path had been elaborately made. Its grass edges were neatly cut and the gravel surface was well weeded, smooth and even. It was soft from recent rains and bore traces of many footprints, among which were several of Maurice's pointing towards the shrubbery. Though it seemed likely he had made them on the night of his death, it was not possible to say so with certainty. Having reached the House they retraced their steps to the car and drove back to Radbury. Superintendent Bowman was in his room.

"I think I'll be able to give you a tentative report later in the day, Mr Bowman," said French, "if you would kindly have these samples compared." He handed over those from the coat and shrubbery. "I take it you have a chemist, or should I send them to the Yard?"

"I'll send them to Bristol. A constable can take them on his bike and bring back the report. What is your conclusion, if I may ask?"

"If you don't mind, I'd rather wait for the test of the samples. Perhaps save me talking through my hat." He glanced at Carter. Bowman looked at him curiously, but made no further comment.

Though he had spoken lightly, French was in no joking mood as he settled down to think over what he had learned. From being clear as crystal or nearly so, the case had become doubtful and puzzling. More and more it looked like foul play, yet foul play would not explain all the facts.

First, what suggested murder?

There were the discrepancies in the accident theory he had already noted: Maurice's and Mrs Belcher's characters, Maurice's apparent deafness on the railway, the episode of the gloves and Mrs Belcher's statement thereon and now the fact that Maurice had lain on his back among the shrubs at the new silo.

Could Maurice have been knocked out among the shrubs and then have been carried to the crossing? This would seem to follow from the new discovery. If so, it was obvious that he could not have made the tracks between the silo and the railway. But since these tracks were undoubtedly made by his shoes, this could only mean that someone else was wearing them. Did this suggestion point the way?

Could the murderer – if it was murder – have somehow enticed Maurice out of Cheddon House, have met him at the shrubbery and killed him by sandbagging or in some other way? Could he have laid the body down among the shrubs, taken off the shoes, put them on his own feet, and carried the body to the crossing? Could he have there hidden the body and – ah yes, this was progress! – could he himself have made the tracks to and from Mrs Belcher's? Could he have then replaced the shoes on the body and laid it on the track?

French was pleased with the theory. It would account for the soil on Maurice's back and for all the footprints. It would account for Mrs Belcher's statement and for Maurice's failure to hear or see the approaching train. It would bring Maurice's actions into accord with his character, and would explain the planting of the gloves – though not how this was done. No doubt it was to call attention to the lady before the footprints at her house disappeared.

A small glow of self-satisfaction crept into French's mind, only to be dispelled by a further devastating idea. He had made a mistake: Maurice had not been murdered among the shrubs. He had been killed by the train. The doctor had been absolutely clear on the point. French whistled soundlessly as he wondered whether all his conclusions were equally false. He returned to the attack.

Maurice had been killed at four-twenty in the morning. But French could not believe that he had only then left Cheddon House. The fact that his bed had not been slept in showed that he had slipped out on the previous evening. What had he been doing during the night?

Sorely puzzled, French began to get the heads of his unsatisfactory argument down on paper. There was nothing like putting a thing in writing to clear the mind. He was interrupted once by a telephone message from police headquarters in Bristol which said that the mould from the coat was identical with that from the shrubbery. This helped French only technically, for he had not doubted it.

Then still another idea flashed into his mind and once again he experienced the excitement of the chase. Perhaps Maurice *had* left Cheddon House in the late evening and his body *had* lain among the shrubs till the morning. He stood up. The matter must be put to the test at once.

"Come along and let's see that doctor again, Carter," he said, trying to speak without eagerness. "Perhaps we can get some more out of him."

Dr Manning had just reached home after his morning round and saw them at once. French realized that the suggestion he was about to make was somewhat delicate, and racked his brains to find the proper approach. When greetings were over he went on: "I'm up against a difficulty in this affair, doctor, and I'm hoping you can help me out. May I ask you to treat what I have to say confidentially for the present?"

Manning agreed, obviously surprised.

"First I'm sure you'll be sorry to hear that there is reason to believe this was no accident. We fear murder."

"Murder?" Dr Manning was clearly taken aback. "Good heavens, Superintendent, that's very distressing. Are you certain?"

"No, sir, but you may help me to certainty."

He shook his head. "I can tell you no more than I've done already."

"You may be able to do so. But first I must say something which seems to question your report. You mustn't take it amiss."

"Go ahead."

"The point is this. In your report you tell us the injuries from the train were fatal: that till the engine struck him Mr Vale was alive."

The doctor nodded without speaking.

"Some evidence we have obtained would seem to clash with that. It suggests that Mr Vale left his house late on the previous evening, that he was then somehow knocked out, that his body was hidden among shrubs for some hours, that it was then carried down and laid on the railway, being run over by the goods at four-twenty."

Amazement and annoyance struggled for mastery on Manning's face. "This is a very astonishing statement, Superintendent. I don't know what your evidence is, but if you mean by 'knocked out' that he was killed, your theory is wrong. He was not killed till the train at four-twenty."

"Quite so: I accept that, Doctor, and there's the problem. How can I reconcile his being knocked out at, say, eleven p.m. and not being killed till more than five hours later?"

Manning shrugged. "Well, how can you?"

French leant forward. "I don't know whether it's possible: you can tell me. I suggest that Mr Vale was seized in the dark and given an injection which made him unconscious, but did not kill him."

"No good: he'd have cried out."

"Not if the assailant knew his job. Think of commando training. Mr Vale could have been held in a lock and the needle shoved into his neck."

"By one person and in the dark? Not likely. A needle isn't a bayonet, you know."

French was staggered. He could visualize Maurice being held in a lock with the assailant's one hand and silenced with the other. Admittedly both these could not be done with one hand. Therefore if one hand had been used to inoculate him, the other would have been required to hold him and he *would* have cried out. Certainly here was a snag. However, time enough for that. Better get all he could from Manning while they were talking.

"What about the drug, Doctor? Is there one that would do the trick?"

"Oh yes, morphia would if your murderer could have got hold of it."

"That difficult?"

"Not to a doctor or perhaps a nurse. Next to impossible to the ordinary public."

"Huh," said French, "not so good for me. But I gather the thing would be possible for two people, one of whom was a doctor or a nurse?"

"Possible I should think, if not very likely."

"Very well, Doctor, one more point, but it's important. Could you find out if it was done?"

Manning had grown much less friendly. "Yes, I suppose so. But it would mean a p-m. Unpleasant for the family."

"I'm sorry, but we couldn't consider that."

"Well, it's up to you. I take it you're pretty sure of your ground? I saw no traces of a needle."

"How could you, sir, with all those injuries? I'll get the order if you'll carry on."

Late that evening French and Bowman received the report. French's theory was correct. Maurice had been drugged by an injection of morphia.

"Murder," French commented grimly; "if Manning's right, by two people, one a doctor or nurse. Who do you put in the running, Super?"

Bowman's reply was unprintable.

– 6 –

"RODNEY'S CONFERENCE"

Shortly before nine next morning French and Carter reached the police station. French had waited on the previous evening while Bowman had rung up the CC, to inform him of the new development. Major Harwood had replied fixing 9.00 a.m. for a conference.

French thought him looking tired and worried as presently he strode into the little office. He greeted French gloomily. "No doubt I should congratulate you on your good work," he announced without enthusiasm, "but though I suspected something wrong, I hoped it wouldn't be murder. Can hardly believe it, you know."

"I'm afraid, sir, there's no doubt."

"Not suggesting there is. You fellows are always pretty sure when you speak. Now, Super, when you're ready we'll go ahead."

They took their places round the table as at the previous meeting. The Major turned at once to French. "I suppose no one knows of your suspicions?"

"Only Dr Manning, and I pledged him to secrecy."

Harwood nodded. "Right, Manning's safe enough. Then the family haven't been told?"

French looked at Bowman, who said they had not.

"H'm." The Major moved uneasily. "Up to me to tell them, I suppose. They'll take it badly. Probably knock the old man out altogether."

"It'll be distressing for them, sir, but we can't help it," Bowman commented.

"Help it? Of course not. Matter of fact they'd prefer to know the truth. Right then, Mr French, go ahead with your story."

French recounted his discoveries, explained the theory he had formed, and told of the confirmation from the post-mortem.

"Good work, good work indeed," Harwood declared handsomely. "Certainly you've not left much room for doubt. But I confess it's a jolt. Couldn't have believed it. No motive, you know."

"I was going to ask you about that, sir," French responded. "You knew the family. Who could have wished for Mr Vale's death?"

"But that's just it. No one! Maurice was a good fellow, quiet and unassuming and kindly. Decent in every way. He hadn't an enemy in the world."

"He must have had one, sir."

"Yes, damn it, I suppose he must. Well, I don't know who it was." The Major's expression grew incredulous. "I tell you I can't even imagine anyone wishing his death."

"Routine will bring it out," suggested French. "At least I hope so."

"Oh yes, you'll get it all right. Now, French, you've put up a good theory and I can see it meets the facts you've established. But I'm hanged if I can understand the murderer's idea. Seems over-elaborate. Why the need for the injection, for instance? Do you see that, Bowman?"

"With the crime committed in the way it was, it would be necessary. But I don't see why that plan was chosen."

"That's it. Couldn't a simpler plan have done the trick equally well? Let's hear you on that, French."

"As I see it, sir, the deceased was rendered insensible and doped before his normal time of going to bed, since his bed was not slept in. Whether this was done in Cheddon House and he was carried out, or whether he was enticed to the shrubbery by some trick and knocked out there is not yet certain. I suspect the latter because his conversation about the Persian film and the torch in his pocket suggest that he meant to go out."

"I think you're right."

"He was not placed on the rails till after half past three, when the last train passed before that which killed him. The marks show that he lay for some time in the shrubbery: I suggest during the whole intervening period."

"We may pass that, eh, Bowman?"

Bowman agreed and French continued: "If murder were not to be suspected, some motive for his leaving the house had to be supplied. A scheme was devised for the purpose. One of Mrs Belcher's gloves was planted in his pocket to draw attention to her and make sure the footprints at her house would be discovered."

"A foul scheme it was," Harwood muttered. "Not only to kill the chap, but to blacken his character. We must get them, French."

"I hope we shall, sir. But continuing. If the deceased visited Mrs Belcher, he would spend some hours there. The supposed accident would not take place therefore till the early morning. The murderer would know the time could be established from marks on the engine."

"Agreed. Yes?"

"If Mr Vale had been murdered when he left Cheddon House, the doctor would at once have exposed the fraud: hence he must be kept alive though helpless, and actually be killed by the train. There were no marks on the wrists or ankles, therefore he had not been tied up. It was difficult to see how he could have been made to drink anything. The injection occurred to me and the p-m showed it had been given. The whole of the elaboration was therefore to support the theory of accident."

"I see the point. You're probably right. What do you say, Bowman?"

"I think there's no doubt it's what happened, and if Mr French hadn't been so wide awake, the murderer might have got off with it."

French thought this generous of Bowman. So often he had been up against jealousy and spite from local officers that it was a pleasure to find a different spirit.

"That's right," agreed Harwood. "Carry on, French, What have you got to work on?"

"Quite a bit, I think, sir. The chief thing is that if the murderer wore Mr Vale's shoes, his feet must not be larger than Mr Vale's. Mr Vale wore eights, which is on the small side. That alone may eliminate a number of possibles."

"Yes, I see that." Major Harwood spoke doubtfully. He did not appear to be pleased with the suggestion. "What else?"

"Well, whoever planned the affair was good at that sort of thing. The murderer had intelligence and probably education, and also a reputation for good planning."

"Huh. Anything more?"

"He must have had a close connection with Cheddon House. To have got Mr Vale out secretly and late at night, he must have known him and his peculiarities, and probably the general circumstances obtaining in the family. I don't see how a stranger could have done it. This of course is not certain, but it's likely."

The Major's face was growing blanker. "It's likely, yes," he admitted shortly. "That all?"

"No, sir, there are still a few points. The murderer's knowledge of the household must have been detailed. He not only knew that Mrs Belcher sat as a model, but he was able to get one of her and of Mr Vale's gloves. We can see how he planted them on the body, but he must have been in quite an exceptional position to plant them in the drawer in Mrs Belcher's bedroom."

Major Harwood made a gesture. "By Jove, yes! I hadn't thought of that. What do you make of it, Bowman?"

"There can't be many people all that applies to," the Super answered slowly. "You're halfway there already, Mr French, if you ask me."

"Yes, that's so. Well, French, still more?"

"Another clue was supplied by Dr Manning. In fact he suggested two. First he said that to have held Mr Vale and prevented him from crying out was a whole-time job for one man, and whoever was doing it couldn't possibly have given the injection. That meant that two people were involved."

Major Harwood brightened up at this. "That should be a help," he declared.

French shook his head. "I'm afraid, sir, the doctor was not correct. It would have been easy for the murderer to have come up behind Mr Vale and knocked him out: I mean stunned him without killing him. He could then have given the injection at his leisure. The mark of both blow and needle would have been destroyed by the engine."

"True."

"There's a point which tends to confirm this," French went on. "The head and neck were badly injured. I suggest the body was placed on the track so that this would occur."

Harwood was again looking worried. "Sounds reasonable," he grunted. "And the doctor's other point?"

"That may be more help to us. Morphia can't be obtained by the public without a prescription. Dr Manning suggested a doctor or perhaps a nurse might be involved."

Major Harwood stared. "I can scarcely imagine anything less likely."

"Dr Manning wasn't necessarily correct, sir. The murderer might have stolen the drug."

Harwood agreed and they continued discussing the matter, though without reaching any more definite conclusion. Then Major Harwood stood up. "I'll go out now to Cheddon and break the news. I expect, French, you'll be interrogating everyone in the house? I'll tell them to await you."

"Thank you, sir. That will ease things for me."

French was interested in the Major's reaction. At their first conference he had wondered if the man had known more than he had divulged, now he again asked himself the question. Harwood had seemed to grow increasingly worried as the tale progressed, and a strange feature of this had emerged. It was the facts which pointed to local knowledge on the murderer's part which had increased his uneasiness. Could he, French wondered, suspect someone at Cheddon?

Then an unpleasant idea occurred to him. Harwood! Surely the respected Chief Constable could not know anything material about the affair? Know anything? French chid himself for not facing the thing. Could Harwood have murdered Maurice Vale?

The CC's position would not preclude the crime. It would not be the first time a senior police officer had gone off the rails. French sat lost in thought. From early in their first conference he had more or less subconsciously formed the idea that Harwood had not wished the truth to come out. True he had called in the Yard, the act of a madman were he guilty. But perhaps in that he couldn't help himself. It appeared to be true that their CID Inspector was down with pneumonia. If Bowman had said he hadn't the staff to handle the affair, the CC could scarcely have refused to obtain help.

Then sanity returned as French realized that the whole of the man's reaction would be accounted for if he were in love with Anne Vale. There was indeed no real reason to suspect him.

"Well, Super," French said to Bowman, who had begun work on his correspondence, "I suppose I can't spend the day at your fire. Cheddon House seems to call. See you later."

Rupert and Rodney were together in the latter's sanctum when French and Carter were shown in. French apologized for troubling them and expressed a suitable regret at the new development. "I'm afraid, gentlemen, we'll later have to take more detailed statements from you and the others. But that can wait. I now want your permission to examine Mr Vale's rooms and papers."

French looked from one to the other, but Rupert answered, "Apply to my brother for whatever you want, Superintendent. I'm not long home and a visitor at that. He's the resident."

"I understand, sir," French said, and turned to Rodney.

"Of course, Superintendent, go where you like. Naturally we'll all help you in every way we can."

"Thank you, sir. One other thing. I should like to know where you obtained your household staff, and references of any members which you may hold."

Rodney shook his head. "I doubt if I can give you that. Lamson has been with us for years, and so has Mrs Felton, the cook. The housemaid is a recent importation and so of course is Nurse M'Candless. I'll have any information that there is turned up."

It sounded well, in fact it could hardly have sounded better. Yet it did not satisfy French. The uneasiness he had noted in Rodney's manner was now more pronounced than ever. It was hard to believe that the man was as ignorant of the affair as he pretended. French could have sworn that if he didn't know the truth, he suspected it. Brigadier Rodney Vale, DSO and bar, was in fact a man to watch.

This determination was abruptly clinched when French cast a glance at his shoes. They were, he believed, eights. He had noted Lamson's shoes when he had opened the door: tens at least. Therefore of the two men who were in the house on the night of the crime, only Rodney need be considered.

In answer to a call from Rodney, Lamson presently arrived to conduct them to Maurice's rooms. With the intention of searching more than the suite, French turned to him. "I wish you'd point out the different rooms as we go up. I may have to move about the house and I'm anxious not to disturb Sir Leigh."

This worked admirably. It appeared that Sir Leigh's, the nurse's, Rupert's and Rodney's rooms were on the first floor and not far apart. Maurice's were on the second or top floor because of the roof light.

"He had five rooms here, sir," Lamson explained: "his sitting-room, bedroom, studio with models' changing-room and store." He led the way through them. "If there's anything else you want, kindly ring and I'll come up."

French thanked him. Then, having signed to Carter to remain where he was, he slipped out of the suite and watched the old man go downstairs. When he disappeared, French followed silently. In a moment he was in Rodney's room.

A glance was sufficient. Rodney's shoes were eights. They were of a slightly narrower fitting than Maurice's. So far as this was concerned, therefore, Rodney could have committed the crime.

He returned to Maurice's suite unnoticed. In the bedroom there was nothing which interested him. The sitting room meant more work. It contained a desk and masses of books and papers. Tidiness was evidently not Maurice's long suit, and letters, circulars, bills and cancelled cheques were heaped together in confusion. French groaned as he contemplated them. He turned to Carter. "Clear that table," he directed resignedly, "and sort these papers into piles as I pass them over."

The work was tedious and unprofitable. The letters were mostly personal: a good many were connected with art and proved that Maurice was recognized as a man of talent. His bank papers showed a competency approaching wealth. Nowhere was there any suggestion of trouble or friction in the man's life.

Of the four letters Lamson had delivered to him on the day of his death, French found three. Two were circulars which had reached the waste-paper basket, the third was about a visit Maurice had apparently been intending to pay to a London artist. Of the fourth letter there was no trace.

In Maurice's engagement book there was no entry for the evening of the tragedy, but on looking back through the pages French came on a note which mildly interested him. It was for Tuesday, 18th September, and read: "9.00 p.m. Rodney's conference." Of course at that date it could have had nothing to do with the man's death, but French wondered what sort of conference could have been necessary between brothers living in the same house.

By the time French had completed a fruitless search of the studio, models' dressing-room – which was only a screened-off corner of the studio – it was close on one o'clock. He swore at having so little to show for his morning's work, but agreed with Carter that sorting papers was hungry work. "We've got to see those servants," he remarked as they drove back to Radbury for lunch, "and I think we ought to meet Selmer and his wife: that's the cousin who runs the farm. We'll take that next."

Accordingly after their meal the two men drove out to Cheddon Bungalow. The door was opened by Pauline.

"Oh yes," she said when French gave his name. "Brigadier Vale told me you were here and I was expecting you. Come in."

The moment she spoke French's interest was aroused. Here surely were the same signs of nervousness, almost of apprehension, which he had noticed in the case of Rodney. It looked as if both had information which was at least embarrassing. He determined to touch lightly on various subjects and note the result.

His efforts had not much success. The embarrassment or apprehension or fear which Pauline so evidently felt did not vary according to the questions asked. It persisted all through the interview, diminishing only when French stood up to take his leave.

He requested information about herself, her family, her marriage and George, checking her answers with Rodney's.

Then he went on to speak of Maurice, and asked whether she knew if he had any enemies. She told him nothing which he had not already known, but he sensed a feeling of liking for Maurice which he had not noticed in Rodney's case. Then he inquired when she had last seen the deceased.

"Not for a couple of days before his death. I generally visit the House at least once a day to have a word with Sir Leigh, but the others are not always there."

"You weren't up at the House on the evening of the tragedy?"

"No, I was here. My husband wasn't very well and I was attending to him."

Having obtained details of George's attack, French thanked her. He said that was all he wanted and asked where he could find George.

"About the farm, but I'm afraid I don't know in what part. If he's not at the farmyard, someone will direct you."

George was with the cowman in the byre, where it seemed a cow was ill. He was obviously worried and asked French to wait while he continued his examination. "Come to my room," he said then. "I want to ring up the vet before he goes out. After that I'll be at your service."

A long conversation followed, in which the animal's symptoms were discussed in detail. At last the vet said he would come out immediately.

"It's a valuable Jersey," George explained, "our best milker and we can't afford to lose her. But that's not what you're interested in. What can I do for you?"

"Just answer a few routine questions, if you please."

"Sit down." He pointed to chairs. "I'll be glad to help in any way I can, but I hope you'll excuse me when the vet comes. That will be in about fifteen minutes."

"I shall not take as long as that. Now, Mr Selmer," and he began his round of questions.

George answered everything readily enough, but with the same indications of uneasiness as were shown by Rodney and Pauline. He gave but little fresh information, most of what he said simply confirming what was already known. The one decisive fact which French learned was from a glance at his feet. They were of a large size, so it was impossible that he could have worn Maurice's shoes.

French returned to the car feeling dissatisfied with his progress. He was working as hard as he could, but with these interviews at least he did not seem to be getting anywhere. Apart from the suggestion – which he could not prove – that Rodney, Pauline and George might be hiding some material fact, he had learned nothing promising. This certainly applied to Rodney and Pauline, but on second thoughts he was not so sure about George. His signs of anxiety might have been due to worry about the cow. French glanced at his watch. It was just half past three.

"Run into Axworth, Carter," he directed. "I don't imagine Maurice went to that cinema, but we'd better make sure."

Axworth, as all know, is a considerable town with a long and wide promenade and a fine pier. French could imagine it black with people in the summer, but at this time of year there were not many in the streets. They entered from the back of the town through a rather mean suburb, but soon reached a broad thoroughfare in which was an ornate cinema.

"We'll try there."

French's card quickly brought him to the office of a polite but slightly anxious manager. "I sincerely hope there's nothing wrong, Superintendent?" he declared as he pulled out chairs and offered cigarettes.

"Nothing connected with you or your cinema," French reassured him. "All I want is a little unusual information. Can you tell me whether Persian scenery comes into any of the films you're showing this week? Or should I say Iranian?"

The manager stared in surprise. "Persian scenery?" he repeated. "Why no; nothing of the kind. I wish we had such a picture. I'm sick to death of Westerns and the London slums."

"I understand it comes into one of the pictures showing this week in Axworth. Perhaps at one of the other houses?"

The manager picked up a folder. "Here are the week's programmes. I'll go through them if you like. I expect I know all the pictures."

"Very kind of you."

The manager was painstaking. It turned out that he had seen all the pictures but one and none of them were remotely connected with Persia. The exception, a gangster tale of Chicago, did not sound promising.

"I'll slip round to the cinema and make sure," French decided. "Most grateful for your help."

"We'd better do the lot, Carter," he went on when they were back in the car. "Some of these programmes might have been unexpectedly changed."

"In that case, sir, Maurice wouldn't have known of it."

"It would seem so, but we must make sure."

It did not take long to inquire at all the cinemas. The result justified the manager. No views of any part of Persia had been shown at any house.

The matter was rather puzzling. Since the story was false, either Maurice or Rodney must have invented it. But why? French could think of no possible motive.

He glanced at his watch. It was just five. "Call at Cheddon House again," he told Carter, who was driving. "We may have time to check up on the staff before they start preparing dinner."

Once again conscientious work drew a blank. Both Lamson and Mrs Felton had been butler and cook respectively for many years and Rodney vouched for their characters. French talked to them and when he found that his own first impressions of them remained favourable, he troubled no further with their pasts.

Nurse M'Candless also struck him as a woman of worth. He could not imagine her mixed up in a murder case, and though he noted the agency through which she had been engaged, he felt that inquiries there would only prove a matter of form.

There was less need for investigation in the case of Susan Stewart, the housemaid, as she was too new an arrival to have developed a murderous interest in the household. All the same he discussed her coming with Lamson, who had engaged her. She had called the day after her predecessor, Molly Crawford, had left, to say that she had met Molly by chance while waiting for a train, and so had learned of the vacancy. She admitted that she had not held such a post before, but she had run her own house for many years and knew all that had to be done. Owing to her husband's recent death she found herself without sufficient funds and was therefore looking for work. It happened that she had lived in Gloucester, in which city Lamson had been brought up, and when she mentioned the names of several people of whom he knew, he had no hesitation in starting her on probation. She had, he considered, proved very satisfactory, and this opinion was endorsed by Rodney. To French she seemed quiet, civil and efficient. He obtained her Gloucester address, as also that to which Molly Crawford had gone, and on reaching the police station rang up the local superintendents, asking that Susan Stewart's statement should be checked and where Molly Crawford had been on the night of the murder.

At the police station he found waiting for him a reply about the Vale succession, which had just come in from the Yard. A man had been to Somerset House and had seen Sir Leigh's father's will. This so fully bore out the information the family had given him that he believed in this one matter at least he had reached bedrock fact.

As that evening he wrote up his notes he felt rather unhappy about the case. He was working hard, but making little progress. When he had finished he read his notes through from the beginning, marking everything which seemed worth further investigation.

One of these items was the entry in Maurice's engagement book for the 18th September, which read: "9.00 p.m. Rodney's conference." As French had already realized, a date some seven weeks prior to the murder made any connection with it unlikely. All the same it was something which had concerned both brothers, and he felt he should know more about it.

Who could tell him? If by any chance it were connected with the tragedy it might be better not to ask Rodney. But might not the conference, whatever it was, have been a family affair? If so, Pauline would be his best hope. On chance therefore he began next morning with a call at Cheddon Bungalow. Pauline was clearly surprised to see him return, but asked him in as before.

"I'm really sorry to trouble you again so soon," he began, "but I find I omitted to get some dates from you – of your marriage and so on. You will understand that we have to make a short life history of everyone connected with our cases. Seldom needed, I admit, but it's the routine."

"That's quite all right, Mr French. I'll tell you anything I can."

Taking out his notebook, French began to add appropriate dates to the events of her life. "I think that's all," he said presently, then ran his finger down a page in his book. "No, just one other point. Do you happen to remember the night of Tuesday, the 18th of September?"

She stared, then shook her head.

"Perhaps if I tell you that it was the night of Brigadier Vale's conference, it will bring it to your memory?"

That he had struck oil French saw instantly, though how literally he did not realize. Pauline seemed to shrink back and a look of absolute horror showed in her eyes. For a moment she was silent, then she stammered, "I don't really know what you mean."

French pressed his advantage. "Oh, come now, Mrs Selmer," he said lightly, "you can't expect me to accept that. You couldn't possibly have forgotten in that short time."

She looked hunted, her eyes turning this way and that as if seeking some way of escape. French decided to bluff. He grinned at her amicably and went on: "You must give me credit for *some* intelligence, you know. I wouldn't have asked you about the meeting if I hadn't known it took place."

Obviously she could not brazen it out. "There – there was a meeting on the date you mention," she answered tremulously. "But it had nothing to do with – this dreadful affair. It was a purely family matter."

"I know that of course," French lied easily. "But I must have your account of it for my notes." Then as she did not speak he went on in a more serious tone: "If you make a mystery of it, Mrs Selmer, you must see that you'll only arouse my suspicions. And if you arouse my suspicions I give you my word that with my Yard training I'll quickly find out all about it. Then I'll ask myself why you wouldn't tell me."

He could see that she felt herself beaten. With an effort she pulled herself together. "Since you put it like that," she said more normally, "I see that I shall have to tell you. But it's a very private matter, and I'd first like your assurance that it will go no further."

"Provided it has nothing to do with the murder, madam, it will be kept an absolute secret."

"I suppose you couldn't say more than that. Well, I'll tell you because I have to. Rodney had made a discovery," and she went on to describe his idea, his researches, and his proposals about buying land and working the oil.

"That was about seven weeks ago," French commented. "Has anything been done about it since?"

"I don't think so. Nothing was decided at the meeting. You understand it was a new and very revolutionary idea, and we all wanted to think it over."

"Was the general feeling for or against the proposal?"

"Speaking for myself, I could really hardly say. The arguments both for and against seemed to me to be strong."

"You didn't give an opinion?"

"No, I said I'd have to think about it."

"And Sir Leigh?"

She seemed to feel this question. "He said it was not a matter for him. He knows, you understand, that he's – very ill."

French nodded. "I'm sorry, madam. And Mr Maurice?"

"Maurice was against it. But of course that was a first reaction."

"Who else was there?"

"Only Major Rupert and George, my husband. Both were in favour. Then there's the Vale sister, Miss Anne Vale, who's in America. She hasn't yet been asked her opinion, but we think it will be favourable."

French, having got more than he could have hoped for, now wanted to set Pauline's mind at rest. He closed his notebook. "I see. Well, Mrs Selmer, I can understand that you didn't want a matter of this kind to become public property." He stood up. "I am very grateful for your help. Now there's just one other thing. I have an appointment, but I want a note of that meeting – just very roughly what took place. Carter, you'd better stay and make it. He won't keep you long, madam, and then the affair will be done with."

He bowed himself out, leaving the understanding Carter to keep Pauline from the telephone. Meanwhile he himself drove to the House and asked for Rodney.

"Sorry, Brigadier, for troubling you again," he began. He was a firm believer in politeness, partly for the pleasanter contacts it made, and partly because it tended to put his subjects off their guard. So he discussed his activities with whimsical detachment till both were comfortably settled, then without further preamble went on: "I'm afraid, sir, you haven't been very straight with me. Why did you keep back all that business about the oil?"

That Rodney was completely taken aback, he was quite unable to hide. He gaped at French with open mouth, at last stammering: "We – we hoped to keep that – a secret. How on earth do you know about it?"

"You need have no fear of publicity," French assured him. "The police know, but no one else. A note among your brother's papers put me on the track, and I persuaded Mrs Selmer to fill in some of the blanks."

Rodney was obviously overcome. French could see him wondering what position to take up and coming to a decision. "Well, I don't know how you managed it, but you're quite right," he admitted. "There's oil under all this area. But for heaven's sake, Superintendent, keep it to yourself. Don't you see what a difference its publication would make to us?"

"I realize it, sir."

"I most sincerely hope you do. With the knowledge confined to the family we could either work the oil ourselves and have the large profits, or do nothing and so preserve our family home. The least hint to outsiders and we would lose both."

"Yes, I see that. I told Mrs Selmer that unless the matter should prove to be connected with the murder, it would be kept an absolute secret, and I now repeat this to you."

Rodney seemed somewhat reassured. "Well, that's something at least, for of course there could be no connection."

French did not comment on this. "Though I have given the promise," he went on, "that does not relieve me from getting the details for my report. Will you please tell me what occurred?"

Rodney was growing more normal. "I don't mind doing that, provided you keep it to yourself. It was one day when I met the engineer of that new silo," and he went on to recount what he had noticed in the pit, his taking of samples, and the assayers' report. Then he said that at the conference he had put the facts before the family with a view to deciding on some action.

"And what was decided?" French asked.

"Nothing, nor did I expect it then. The matter was too important to settle off-hand. It required thinking over."

"Yes, I see that. How was the idea received?"

"Speaking generally, Maurice was against doing anything and Rupert and George in favour of it. My father said it wasn't a matter for him and Pauline couldn't make up her mind. Anne has not yet been asked."

"And what has been done since?"

"Nothing. We have not seen our way clear. Personally I have felt that as anything of the kind would greatly distress my father, we should postpone action during the short time he is likely to be with us."

Eminently reasonable, and in so far as French could judge, true. Directly he had learned of this matter of the oil and of Maurice's opposition, he had seen what a strong motive for murder it gave Rodney. But now that he had heard Rodney on the subject, he was less sure. Unless the Brigadier was a consummate actor, Maurice's opposition to his plans had not been vital. Having obtained the usual details of names and dates, he thanked Rodney and drove back to Radbury.

– 7 –

EVIDENCE FROM THE DECEASED

To Pauline the days following the tragedy were the most terrible of her life.

There was first her sense of loss in Maurice's death. She had never been exactly fond of him, but his quiet friendship and kindly good will had been pleasant and helpful.

The actual cause of the loss, the fact that he had died from somebody's malice, appalled her. These things happened of course, but to others and at a distance. The deed itself was hideous enough, but its horror was aggravated by the publicity that followed. Why must people be such ghouls? They could not keep the grounds clear of reporters, crowding in like vultures in search of carrion for their obscene public. Then there was the inquest. Rodney said it would be adjourned and over in a few minutes. But it would have a second part. That might be worse, ten thousand times worse, than publicity. If awkward questions were asked, if terrible suspicions were aroused, what further horrors might they not have to endure?

Pauline would not admit it to herself, but what was really gnawing at her heart was fear. Though again and again she reminded herself of Rodney's uprightness and genuine goodness, the demon of doubt was there. She could not forget his expression when he had looked at Maurice, the glances of absolute hatred which she from time to time had surprised. There was no doubt that Maurice was standing in the way of the oil development scheme, upon which she knew Rodney had set his heart. It could not be, she told herself in her saner moments, and yet the fear remained.

She wondered had the idea occurred to French, and shivered. French she found absolutely terrifying! He was polite, pleasant even, apparently anxious to avoid giving her pain. Yet never had she met anyone more persistent, more utterly relentless. She felt that once he got hold of an idea he would not drop it till he had squeezed out every single one of its ramifications and its entire bearing and significance. He was, not exactly dishonest, but shrewd to a point approaching it. See how he had wormed out from her about Rodney's oil meeting. He had made her think he had known about it, but he hadn't known. She supposed in his dreadful job such methods were necessary, but it revolted her to have them applied to herself.

She would have given half her income to know just what he thought of the case. But her contact with him told her that she would be as likely to get the moon. These two men were working away, in the house, about the grounds, asking this question and that, but there was never an indication as to where it was all leading. What had they discovered? Above all, did they suspect Rodney? There was no hint of it in their manner, but then from what she had read, there wouldn't be. They would carry on, calmly and normally and politely, day after day, and then quite suddenly and without any warning they would strike. Beyond such a disaster Pauline refused to imagine. What might follow was too appalling.

The strain was getting on all their nerves and tempers began to show frayed. Rodney was like a cat on hot bricks, and George had grown more irritable and was inclined to make excuses for extra glasses of whisky. Rupert, who tended towards aloofness where family matters were concerned, was markedly on edge. Lamson, who of course was an old man, had gone completely to pieces. Even the new maid, Susan, was affected. Sir Leigh had taken the affair hard and was visibly weaker. In fact only the redoubtable Ulsterwoman, Nurse M'Candless, had preserved her normal cool efficiency, standing like a rock amid the surrounding unrest.

Pauline went up to the House as soon as Carter left her after that disastrous interview about Rodney's meeting. Rodney was alone in his own room. She sank into a chair. "Oh Rodney, was he here?" she breathed, as absently she lit a cigarette.

He rose and stood with his back to her, staring out of the window. "Just gone. They know about the oil."

She made a gesture of regret. "What will you say to me, Rodney? I'm afraid I told them."

"So he indicated. Don't worry, you couldn't help it. They trick you, and ordinary people aren't able to stand up against them. It's their job."

"I didn't really mean – "

"Of course not. Don't give it another thought. Besides, it was certain to come out. I'd have had to tell them myself."

"You think so?"

"Certain of it. Nothing can be kept secret in these inquiries. Besides, what harm their knowing if they keep it to themselves, and French has promised to do that."

"I know: he promised me. But can you trust him?"

Rodney jerked about impatiently. "Hang it all, old girl, how do I know? Anyhow, we've no choice."

"He seemed honest, I thought."

"I was very keen on it," Rodney went on, not listening to her, "and now I don't care a tinker's curse whether we ever see the blessed oil or whether there's any oil to see. Somehow it doesn't seem worthwhile."

"I know. I feel that way too." She looked at him, her fear sharp in her mind. She couldn't speak of it; yet she must. Some internal urge drove her on. "There's one absolutely – absolutely ghastly thought has occurred to me," she said somewhat shakily. "Rodney, they couldn't – they *couldn't* – suspect you?"

Rodney laughed mirthlessly. He swung round from the window. "Couldn't they?" and his voice was sharp. "It's about the one thing certain in this damned mess. Suspect me? I'll say they suspect me."

Pauline gave a moan.

"How could they do anything else?" Rodney went on harshly. "They know about the oil, they know about the succession, they know or can guess that Maurice was blocking the thing. What more obvious than that I should eliminate him?"

"But you weren't out during that night?"

"How do you know? I could have been. Look," he seemed to warm to the subject, "it's quite simple. I could easily have put a sleeping draught into Maurice's whisky, then during the night have gone to his room and knocked him out. Remember his room's the furthest away, and with the door shut the blow couldn't have been heard even if nurse or the pater were awake. Then I could have carried him to the crossing and laid him on the line." He paused. "I didn't, in case you'd like to know, but I could have."

"Oh, Rodney," she protested.

"I didn't, but I don't see how I can prove it. And it's not facts, but proofs, that matter in a court of law."

Pauline shivered. "Oh, Rodney," she repeated, "for heaven's sake don't mention courts."

"No, I suppose that's premature. Oh well, Pauline, let it alone. If he arrests me, he arrests me, and that's all there is to it. George all right again?"

The inquest was held that afternoon in a room in Radbury. Both Rodney and George had assured her that she need not attend, but she felt she must be there. It was not merely out of respect for Maurice. She felt she must see for herself the bearing of those concerned, and hear if anything was said which could indicate their views about Rodney.

But from the dry impersonal proceedings she learned nothing whatever. The coroner was a stranger to her, a precise legal-looking man, who conducted the affair adequately, but as if sunk in the last extreme of boredom. He elected to sit with a jury. The jurors were empanelled. The railway ganger described his finding of the body. Sergeant Dutton told of its conveyance to the mortuary and of his asking Dr Manning and Brigadier Vale to inspect it. The doctor gave evidence identifying it from the birthmark and proving that death was due to the railway injuries. Rodney recounted Maurice's disappearance from Cheddon House. The coroner then amazed everyone not in the know by saying that he understood additional evidence might shortly be available, and to give the police time to carry on their inquiries, he would adjourn the proceedings till further notice. Not a single word or glance relieved or confirmed Pauline's fears.

Nor had Rodney been able to form any opinion as to the official view. Pauline could see that he was apprehensive, but he dismissed the subject by saying that they couldn't do anything about it, so why worry? Logical, but unhelpful.

Later that day Rupert surprised her. While always polite, he had never been exactly friendly. Now she learned that he was more observant and sympathetic than she had supposed. He came up and spoke with feeling. "Look, Pauline, you're worrying yourself sick about nothing. I know what you're afraid of. Well, you needn't be. Rodney's as innocent as the babe unborn and no one could suspect him." She was a little shocked to have her thought stated so bluntly, but she felt that Rupert had meant to be kind and she warmed to him accordingly.

On the heels of the inquest came another ordeal, that of the funeral. To Pauline's immense relief Rodney had decided it was to be private: a difficult decision in view of the standing of the family and the tragic circumstances of the death. It took place in the Radbury Cemetery, and there on a hill overlooking the estuary Maurice's body reached its final resting-place. Pauline found the scene distressingly poignant, and was thankful when she and George were once more back in the Bungalow.

Her depression that night was greater than ever. For hours she lay wakeful and tossing, only drifting off into a heavy sleep when a faint light was showing in the east. She woke with the thought of Rodney still uppermost in her mind.

So, heavy with fear, the days began slowly to drag by.

On the Sunday of that weekend French called first at the police station. There two items of news had come in. The statements of both Nurse M'Candless and the new maid, Susan Stewart, had been verified. The nurse had been known for many years to the agency which supplied her. She held the highest testimonials, and the manageress vouched for her character in every way. Mrs Stewart's statements as to her having lived in Gloucester and the death of her husband were also true. This being what French had expected to hear, he did not consider himself much further on from the information.

He devoted his morning to bringing his notes up to date and making another comprehensive survey of the case. Almost invariably he had found that when the first obvious inquiries had been made, time was saved rather than lost by sitting still and thinking. A comfortable armchair and a pipe – or better still a wakeful night in bed – and a leisurely browse over the facts usually bore a worthwhile harvest.

He was impressed by the story of the oil. Many factors in the case had pointed to Rodney, but there had been no suggestion of a motive. But if Rodney wished to develop the oil and Maurice was blocking his plan, there might be a strong one. In this case Rupert and George would be equally interested. Perhaps not equally, as the plan was so to speak Rodney's child, but quite sufficiently to account for the murder. Rupert moreover bore, or had borne, a shady reputation. But on French's present information both Rupert and George were innocent. At the time of the crime Rupert had been in London, and George was ill and in Pauline's care, as well as being unable to wear Maurice's shoes. French noted that Rupert's London alibi must be thoroughly tested.

However, continuing on the information he had. If Rupert and George were out of it, that left Rodney. French looked up again the evidence against him.

1. Rodney could have worn Maurice's shoes.
2. Rodney had the necessary ingenuity, cool courage, resourcefulness and physical strength.

3. Rodney had the necessary knowledge about Maurice, Mrs Belcher, Cheddon House and the district.
4. Rodney had a motive which might well have been overwhelming.
5. Last, but by no means least, no one but Rodney had these essentials.

French almost writhed as he considered whether he should or should not recommend an arrest. Of course this was theoretically a matter for the Chief Constable, but French knew that if he put up a sufficiently strong case, Major Harwood would have to act. Had he then such a case?

He turned to what could be said in Rodney's favour. A charge against him must have the three time-honoured essentials for a conviction: motive, opportunity, and an actual connection with the crime. But here motive would not be proved unless there was evidence that Maurice was holding up the oil scheme, and so far there was none. Opportunity would not be established unless the whole scheme could be explained, and French did not know how Rodney could have planted the gloves in Mrs Belcher's bedroom. Of actual connection with the crime there was no evidence whatever.

French whistled tunelessly. On the whole he doubted if he had enough for a conviction. This view was strengthened when he remembered that he had not yet discovered how Maurice had been induced to go out into the shrubbery. No, he told himself, more work would be necessary before he could ask the CC for a conference.

Having reached this conclusion, he decided to take the afternoon off. Sunday in any case was a bad day for any but the most urgent inquiries. Unhappily it was uninviting out of doors, cold and windy and raw, though not actually raining. But he set out with Carter for a tramp along the cliff to Portnore. From here they had fine views. The mud-coloured waters of the estuary with its racing tides were flecked with white, and for once the Welsh coast was clear and sharply defined. A large steamer was nosing up towards Avonmouth, followed at some little distance by a coaster. They enjoyed the complete change of tramping the rough path and fighting the wind, and Carter made an original remark about cobwebs. Then, after a highly satisfactory tea at Portnore they returned by road, striking up over the hills into Radbury.

But they could not keep clear of the case for long. On reaching the hotel they found that Rodney had been ringing up. French quickly called back.

"I remembered at the funeral that I'd omitted to tell you something else about this affair," Rodney explained. "If you care to come over I can see you at any time."

"No peace for the wicked, Carter," French declared. "Get out the car."

"It's with regard to that matter of the oil," said Rodney when they had found chairs. "A rather mysterious affair really," and he showed French the anonymous letter he had received accusing the maid, Molly Crawford, of spreading tales about his discovery.

"You hadn't spoken of the matter to any outsider?" French asked.

"Absolutely not, and that goes for the rest of us as well. We all realized that if the least whisper got about our hopes would be gone."

French was keenly interested. Here was something new in the case: a trace for the first time of an unknown. To have written the letter, someone outside the family must have been aware of the discovery. But who, and how had he learned it? For a moment it seemed that Rodney's conclusion must be correct, that the girl had listened at the door.

But further thought showed that this was unlikely. If a rumour of the kind were started it would spread like wildfire. The local police were always well in touch with current gossip, and some one of them could scarcely have failed to hear the tale. But none had. Any such whisper would have been at once reported. It was almost certain, therefore, that the girl Crawford was innocent.

This brought French back to his first conclusion. If the girl were not involved, some outsider *had* learned of the discovery. But why should this person falsely accuse the girl? Why indeed should he wish Rodney to be aware of his knowledge? Would the secret not have been more valuable to him if his possession of it were unsuspected?

Gradually French's belief in the existence of the outsider grew fainter. At last it vanished altogether. Another idea took its place.

What if Rodney himself had written the note? It was quite easy to guess his motive. French himself had fallen into the trap. The letter would postulate an outsider in the know. If Rodney were planning the murder it would be of the first importance to him that the existence of such a person should be established. It would stultify the argument that only he himself had the knowledge for the crime.

All the same, inquiries must be made. French must himself interview this Molly Crawford. He must search for the typewriter, which was old and worn. He must go into the thing as carefully as if he believed it genuine. He turned back to Rodney.

"You'll have to excuse me, Brigadier, if I say that I think you should have told me this before. Because of the time that has elapsed the writer of this note may be harder to trace."

"I admit you're right and I'm sorry, Superintendent. I can only say that I was so upset during our previous conversation that it slipped my memory."

"Very well, sir, we needn't discuss it further. I'll see this Molly Crawford without delay."

A call to the Bath police elicited the fact that the young woman had a job in one of the local hotels, and next morning French drove over to interview her. He was favourably impressed by her appearance and manner. He questioned her keenly, and at last came to the conclusion that she was innocent of Rodney's charge. She declared, and he believed her, that she could not have discussed Rodney's possible discovery with anyone because she had not known of it. This call of French's was the first intimation of it she had had.

"Well, Miss Crawford, that's all I want to ask you, and thanks for what you've told me. Just one other question. Were there any typewriters at Cheddon House in your time?"

She stared at him so shrewdly that he wondered if she had guessed what was in his mind. "Two, sir," she answered. "One a Remington portable of Miss Anne's, Miss Vale's, I mean. The other was also a portable, a Corona, I think, of Mr Rodney's."

"Were they the only two who could type?"

"I think so. Neither was very good at it, for I can type a bit myself and I know."

"Thank you."

It was not likely, if Rodney had written the letter, that he would have used a machine in the house. From detective stories everyone knew that a machine could be identified from its script. However both must be tested. He went back to Cheddon House and told Lamson to bring all the machines in the house. He brought only the two mentioned and neither had been used for the letter.

Then another and more likely reason occurred to him why Rodney should have been the writer. The letter accused Molly Crawford of conduct which, if proven, must result in her dismissal. Could this have been Rodney's intention?

Why might he have wished her to be sacked? What if she unwittingly held information which might serve as a pointer to the murderer? If Rodney were guilty and thought she might prove a danger, he would get her out of the house as quickly as possible. It was a curious way of doing it – the way of an ingenious planner? – but French did not know that he could suggest a better.

It seemed a pity to spend time going back to Bath, but he felt he could do no less. He had lunch with Carter in a pub in Keynsham and by two-thirty they were once again at the hotel. There, having first enlisted Molly's sympathy, he put her through an extremely detailed examination. But entirely without result.

The clue seemed to be petering out and French felt that at this early stage in the inquiry he could give it no more time. Having noted that search for the typewriter must be made, he felt free to turn to the next item of his programme: the checking of Rupert's alibi. This, though unpromising, had to be done, and as there were several things he wanted to see to at his home, he felt the present a propitious opportunity. Since missing his youngest's birthday party, Carter also had been full of dark hints.

Rupert had given him the names of the men with whom, after the reunion, he had gone to the nightclub, and next day French saw them all, together with the staffs of both assemblies. The result was conclusive beyond the slightest possibility of doubt. Major Rupert Vale had been in London on the night of the murder, and therefore was no longer a figure of interest in the case.

Negative information, but still information and so a step forwards towards the goal. As that evening French sat in the train on his way back to Radbury, he felt that at least an obstruction had been removed from his path.

It was nearly eleven when they reached the hotel. There a message from Bowman was waiting for him. Some fresh information had come in and he would like to see French first thing in the morning.

"That's what we get for going away," French grumbled. "We sweat around here for days and nothing happens, but as sure as we take a run home the fun starts."

"We could do with a bit more dope all the same."

"How right you are! Well, at least he hasn't asked us to go tonight. Sufficient unto the day."

Next morning they overtook Bowman on the way to the police station. "I've got something I think'll interest you," he greeted them, "a letter." On the table in his room there lay an envelope. "I left it for you to open," he explained as they found chairs.

French looked his question. The Super held out his cigarette case, then leaned back in his chair.

"Late yesterday afternoon we had a visit from Mr Robert Fielding, the manager of the local branch of the City and Southern Bank. He had been in Manchester for a few days and had somehow missed seeing the news of Mr Vale's death. He read of the inquest today on the way from Paddington. This reminded him that on what must have been the day before his death Maurice had called at the bank and handed him a letter, asking him to put it in the safe. Mr Fielding brought it over."

French glanced at the envelope. It was of the kind he had seen in Maurice's desk and the writing appeared to be Maurice's. It was heavily sealed and bore the words: "Robert Fielding, Esq. City and Southern Bank, Radbury. Please keep this letter till I call for it. If anything happens to me hand it to the police."

French swore. "Then he expected what was coming to him!"

"Looks like it."

"What about prints, Mr Bowman?"

"We'll try, of course, but I don't expect much. Don't you think we might open it first?"

French nodded, then slit the envelope with his knife and manoeuvred out two sheets and an envelope. Again using his knife, he flattened the sheets on the table.

The first was on the Cheddon Hall headed paper, and was written in what French again believed was Maurice's hand. It read:

THE CHIEF OF POLICE, Radbury.

If you receive this letter, something serious will have happened to me. The enclosed came by first post this morning. I don't know who wrote it.

Over six weeks ago, on the evening of Tuesday, 18th September, to be exact, my brother Rodney called the family together to tell us of his discovery. He proposed to buy up the surrounding land and work the oil. I objected, Rupert and George Selmer approved, and my father and Mrs Selmer reserved judgment. I don't know who else knew, but it looks as if others must have been taken into confidence.

I thought first of showing the letter to Rodney, then decided to try an experiment. I asked him to accompany me this evening to a non-existent film in Axworth. He refused on the ground that he already had an engagement. I felt then that I must know the truth, so said no more, determining to act on the letter. I therefore propose to keep the appointment.

MAURICE VALE.

The second sheet was of quarto size, one of what is usually called White Bank typing paper, thin and used for carbons. Both letter and envelope bore the date of Saturday, 2nd November, and would therefore have been delivered by the first post on the Monday of the murder. It bore no address. It was typed, with a number of mistakes, as if by an amateur.

Mr Maurice Vale

SIR,
I have to inform you that your brother, Brig. Rodney Vale, has discovered that there is oil beneath your estate and is secretly promoting a company to buy up the neighbouring land and work the deposit. If you and your father act at once you may be able to stop this.

You can obtain proof of what I say by being at the shrubs near where Mr Arrow is excavating for his new silo at 11.00 p.m. on Monday next, 4th inst. Your brother is meeting an engineer there at that hour to take samples of the soil for examination.

I am writing you because I don't want Radbury spoiled by oil wells.

AN OLD RESIDENT.

Bowman had come round and was reading over French's shoulder. He swore in his turn. "Pretty thin, that. I'm surprised Maurice fell for it."

"I don't suppose he did really," said French. "He wanted to be sure about his brother, and what could he do but keep the appointment?"

"Damn it all," Bowman growled, "that's a new light to me on Maurice. He suspected Rodney."

"He was doubtful of him, at all events. Well, if he was right, Rodney must have written this. It's certainly from the murderer."

Bowman stooped lower over the paper. "If Rodney typed it, we should get the machine. It's worn and should be easy to identify."

"As a matter of fact I'm nearly sure it's the same machine that did the letter regarding the maid talking about the discovery. I seem to remember that twisted 's'."

"H'm. Believe you're right. We'll soon see."

He turned over the pages of the dossier and laid the letters together. The scripts were obviously the same.

"That should be a help," French observed. "But what about prints, Super, before this one gets smudged?"

"I'll get it looked over." Bowman touched a bell and sent out the papers. "I've thought about Rodney quite a bit," he went on, "and I'm not satisfied. I just can't see him guilty of a crime like this. Not of course that I know him very well. But the CC's very intimate with them all, and I know he takes the same view."

"That's interesting, Mr Bowman, because I've been considering asking for a conference to put up the case for arresting Rodney."

Bowman looked up sharply. "I didn't know you'd got as far as that. Think it's a true bill?"

"I've not made up my mind," French admitted. "I'm sure that technically we've enough for an arrest, but I'd rather have something nearer proof."

"The CC will want to hold off as long as possible."

"I realize that. Hence my indecision."

"This letter may settle the hash."

"It settles three problems right away, but it raises a whole dose of others. It accounts for the fourth letter Maurice received that morning, which I couldn't find. It tells us that Rodney was speaking the truth when he said Maurice had asked him to go to a cinema. I confess I hadn't believed that."

"It looked suspicious," Bowman admitted.

"I was wrong and Rodney was right. Third, it tells us what took Maurice out of the house so secretly, and why he went to that clump of bushes. That was a proper puzzle. Incidentally it tells us the time of the assault."

Bowman whistled soundlessly as if in thought. "If the same machine was used to type both letters it points to the same writer for each. You thought Rodney wrote the first?"

"I thought he might have done so."

"Do you think he wrote the second?"

French moved uneasily. "That's really the larger question, isn't it? If he's guilty he wrote it; if not, I don't see how he could have."

Bowman nodded. Both men sat in silence for some moments, lost in thought. Then French said slowly: "What strikes me is, if the letter was not Rodney's, how did the writer know about the oil?"

"That applies to the first letter as well."

"I know it does."

"One of the family may have talked."

"I doubt it. They were very close about the affair because it was in their interest. A whisper and their profits were gone."

"What about putting it up to Rodney?" French thought this over. "It might bring the matter to a head. Before I do that I ought to have a warrant in my pocket."

It was Bowman's turn to consider. "I don't think it would be necessary," he said at last. "He'd know he couldn't get away."

"He might commit suicide."

"That would show a regrettable laxity on the part of the police," Bowman said dryly. "But it's what the CC would prefer."

French grinned. "I believe you. A smooth passage for him and the sack for me. Quite a scheme for the Somerset police."

"Human nature and that. But seriously, French, you could scarcely expect a warrant on the facts you have, and if you get more facts you can always ring up and the needful would be there in minutes."

"Right, Super, pulling your leg. I'll go out and see Rodney now. I'd like a copy of the letter, please."

History presently repeated itself. The drive to Cheddon House, the reception by Lamson, the stately progress to Rodney's room, the polite salutations and the apologies for still another visit. Then French got to business. He explained how the letter came into the possession of the police and handed over the copy. Rodney read it with an expression of amazement which rapidly turned to dismay.

"But it's not true!" he cried as his eyes passed along the lines. "There's not a word of truth in it from beginning to end! I wasn't doing anything about the oil and I certainly did not make an appointment with any engineer. The whole thing's a tissue of lies!"

"I fancied so," French answered smoothly, "but it still leaves some questions to be answered. I don't mean to be offensive, but can you prove your statement? Who wrote the letter? How did he learn his facts? Things like these. There's quite a bit to be cleared up."

Rodney had paled somewhat and was obviously nervous. "I realize that, of course," he agreed. "I didn't leave the house on that evening, but I don't see how I can prove it."

"When your late brother asked you to go to the film, did you reply that you had another engagement?"

Rodney moved unhappily. "Well, yes, I did. It wasn't true. I only said it to soften down my refusal."

French nodded. "I follow. It might be helpful if you would mention in detail how you spent the evening in question. Now you told me," he flicked over the pages of his notebook, "that you and the deceased and the nurse dined together at seven-thirty and went into the lounge for coffee about eight. You sat there reading till about eight-thirty, when Mr Vale left the room saying he wished to look at something in his studio. Is that all correct, sir?"

"Perfectly correct."

"Then would you please complete the story. What happened after half past eight?"

Rodney did not at once reply, giving the impression of a man in thought. "I can't recall that I did anything particular," he said at last. "I read for most of the evening.

About ten-thirty, according to custom, I went up to say good night to my father: he goes to sleep early. After that I came down again, had a nightcap and went to bed."

"What time did you go to bed, sir?"

"I don't think I could say. About eleven I should think. I've rather a weakness for reading in bed."

"Near enough. Did anyone see you after you left Sir Leigh's room?"

"I don't think so."

"You got yourself the nightcap?"

Rodney made a sudden gesture. "No, by Jove, Superintendent, I forgot that. Lamson brought it in. He can tell you I was here."

"That's good. About what time?"

"When I came down from my father. I was with him about a quarter of an hour. That would make the drink about a quarter to eleven."

French closed his notebook. "Well, that's the lot. I suppose I needn't ask you my other two questions: who wrote the letter and how did he learn the facts?" Rodney was, or seemed to be, completely mystified. He could make no suggestion. French thanked him, trying to give the impression that he was satisfied. When being shown out he asked Lamson for a word. They went to the butler's pantry.

"I'm trying, for my report," French explained, "to make a statement of what everyone did on the night of the tragedy, from half past eight onwards. Will you please say what you did?"

Lamson was a good witness. The events of that evening seemed to be burnt into his mind. After seeing Maurice go upstairs at about half past eight, he sat reading in his pantry for some time, listened to the nine o'clock news and so on. About ten he went round the house, seeing that all doors and windows were properly fastened. He was then occupied with small routine jobs, one of which was to take Rodney a tray with whisky and soda. He always did that after Rodney came down from Sir Leigh; that was about a quarter to eleven. After that he had a small nightcap himself in his pantry and went up to bed about eleven.

"Between half past eight and the time you reached your bedroom, did you see any member of the household other than when you took the whisky to Brigadier Vale?"

"I saw the nurse and Mr Rodney, sir."

"Oh? When was that?"

"Just before I went to bed. After I had my drink I went up to the first floor as I remembered I had not closed the windows of one of the spare rooms and I went in to do that. I saw them through the door."

"What were they doing?"

"The nurse crossed the landing from Sir Leigh's room to her own. As she closed her door Mr Rodney came up from the hall and went into his own room."

If true, this was vital. If Rodney was walking up the stairs in Cheddon House at eleven, he could not have been in the shrubbery at the silo. French wondered could he establish the time more accurately.

Lamson was sure of his statement. He had come downstairs again after seeing Rodney to make sure that all the lights were out and he had noted the time.

French went on to Nurse M'Candless. She was equally sure of her facts. She remembered seeing Rodney coming upstairs as she was crossing the landing from Sir Leigh's room to her own, but she did not speak to him as she had entered her room before he reached the landing. She did not think he had seen her. She also remembered the time. It was just eleven.

Following his own motto "Be Thorough!" French saw Mrs Felton and Susan Stewart before leaving, but neither could help him. Both had gone to bed that night before eleven and had seen no one about the house.

He was puzzled by this testimony and sat down in Lamson's pantry to think it over. It now looked as if Rodney was innocent of the attack on Maurice. If that were so, no one who was at Rodney's meeting could have knocked Maurice out. On the other hand no one who was not at the meeting could have had any motive. This was equivalent to concluding that Maurice could not have been murdered. French writhed as he realized that his reasoning must contain some gigantic flaw.

But was he right in all this? Was Rodney necessarily innocent after all? Suppose after going openly to his bedroom he had slipped silently down again and hurried to the shrubbery? He need only have been ten or fifteen minutes late, and he would doubtless have counted on Maurice waiting during that period. The hall door was a large heavy affair which might be noisy to open, but there was a side door leading direct into the garden.

French examined the side door. It was fastened by a mortice lock and the key was on the inside. French locked and unlocked, opened and closed it. It made no sound. He tip-toed up and downstairs. No tread creaked.

Was this the solution, and was Rodney's going to his room at eleven a precaution taken against the possible discovery of the letter to Maurice? French did not know and swore impotently.

As he sat despondently in the car on the way back to Radbury, wondering what he should say to the CC at their next meeting, a devastating idea shot into his mind. Why, an outsider *did* know about the oil! Several outsiders, he could not say how many! He sat rigid, lost in wonder as to how he could have overlooked anything so obvious. There was no need to consider a possible drunken indiscretion on George's part or keyhole snooping on Molly Crawford's. Rodney himself had given the thing away. Rodney had openly stated that he had done so. And French – and presumably everyone else – had missed the implication.

The agent to whom Rodney had sent his samples! The assayers who eventually received them! Again French marvelled how he had forgotten them.

The agent knew that the samples came from Rodney and he knew where Rodney lived. The report of the assayers passed through his hands. A very elementary putting together of two and two would have told him what was at stake.

And what of the assayers? They would recognize that the ugly lumps of clay were valuable as solid nuggets of gold. A scheme could easily have been devised to obtain from the agent his employer's name. A visit to the address would reveal the silo workings as the only deep excavation in the area. If Rodney could secretly obtain samples, so could others.

There was no doubt that several people could have known of the oil. *But*, and here French experienced another check, none of these people would want to murder Maurice. All they could do would be to blackmail the family for a share in the profits or to buy ground in the district, knowing that the value of this would soar when the working started. Neither of these actions seemed probable. Each would require a much more detailed knowledge of the family and circumstances other than either agent or assayers would be likely to have.

All the same here was a possible line of progress and he dared not neglect it. In point of fact he did not neglect it. He went back to town and made an exhaustive investigation into the circumstances of all concerned, with particular reference to their location on the night of the murder. At last he was convinced. Not one of those in question could have been near Radbury on the fatal night.

Disgruntled and very despondent, he returned three nights later with Carter to Radbury. Once again shortly before eleven they reached the hotel. Once again a message from the police was awaiting them. Cheddon Bungalow was on fire and Superintendent Bowman had gone out there. Would French care to follow?

– 8 –

PAULINE UP AGAINST IT

As time dragged slowly on Pauline's distress grew, if not less, at least somewhat blunted. Whatever the future might hold for them, no blow had yet fallen. At times she thought that every day which passed without disaster was an item of increasing hope, then when depression returned she felt that the forces against them were only building up for the kill. French was still at Radbury, but she had no idea what he was doing or what direction his inquiries were taking. Presumably he had not yet reached a conclusion.

Though she tried to put it out of her thoughts, she knew very well what she meant by a conclusion. He had not so far found evidence to incriminate Rodney. And it was every day which had passed without Rodney's arrest that had seemed to her the item of increasing hope.

She was amazed by what she had learned of the crime. As a result of the police inquiries a good deal had leaked out, and she had heard from Rodney that Maurice had been rendered unconscious during the late evening, and carried down and laid on the railway about four in the morning. She had also heard of his alleged visit to Mrs Belcher, as well as of the extraordinary business of the gloves.

This Mrs Belcher episode in fact did more to relieve her anxiety about Rodney than anything else in the case. It was

Rupert who pointed out its significance. "You think that Rodney might have done poor old Maurice in to get the oil scheme going," he said in his uncompromising way when one day they met and were chatting in the grounds. "Well, you may or may not be right, but I can tell you one thing: Rodney would never have blackened Maurice's character. Not in a thousand years. If the murderer faked evidence to prove that Maurice spent the night with Mrs Belcher, then the murderer was not Rodney."

Then Pauline surprised herself. She had never liked Rupert, but now she felt a warm rush of feeling towards him. "Oh, Rupert, what a comfort you are!" she exclaimed. "Of course you're right. I'm ashamed of myself for having had doubts." After this she felt happier, but gradually she saw that unless French was of the same opinion it would not help Rodney, and of course French could not know his character as they did.

While she thus remained concerned about Rodney, she was gradually becoming, if not anxious, at least a good deal puzzled about George. The tragedy seemed to have been a great shock to him. Of course some such reaction was to be expected, for after all Maurice was his cousin. But he had taken the affair much more to heart than she would have expected. He was more on edge than any of them. His temper had become almost unendurable, and he drank so much that on most evenings he was slightly fuddled. From something Rodney said she imagined he had noticed it too, but she did not care to discuss George with Rodney and so did not learn his views.

So often had she pondered on what could have brought this about, that it was almost inevitable she should at last begin to wonder whether George could know more about the affair than he pretended. Could he by any chance know who was guilty? Some embarrassing knowledge, she thought, was just the thing to account for his condition. Watching him, she gradually came to the conclusion that what he was really suffering from was fear. He had some knowledge, she felt sure, which made him afraid. What could it be?

Then a more terrible idea flashed into her mind. Her blood ran almost cold as she asked herself could George have been himself concerned in the affair?

With sinking heart she thought this over. But soon she grew reassured. That was the evening on which George had been ill. From seven in the evening till one in the morning, off and on, she had sat beside his bed. He could not therefore have been out of the house. Of what then was he afraid?

Obviously he could not have had anything to do with the knocking out of Maurice. But suppose someone else had done that, could George have carried him to the railway? She was asleep before two. Could he have got up and gone out without disturbing her?

She was doubtful, but on the whole she thought he could. Though their beds were side by side, they did not touch nor did they creak. But could George have recovered sufficiently to do such heavy work? The illness was real. It did not need her nurse's training to tell her that. Besides, Dr Manning had seen him and had taken the thing seriously. On the other hand he was a lot better when she went to bed about one.

Had Pauline known about the footprints she would have been a good deal easier in her mind, but she did not know. With the information she had she concluded that it would have been just possible for George to have made the journey. With horror she saw that if he had laid Maurice on the rails, he would be the actual murderer.

Then her horror increased till she felt sick. Could George and Rodney have conspired to carry out the affair jointly? Could Rodney have knocked Maurice out, and then later could George have carried him to the line? George could have had a motive, indeed she saw that he had one, for had not Rodney said that the profits of the oil scheme were to be divided equally among the members of the family?

For a time she was filled with despair, then common sense reasserted itself. There were two reasons why this idea was absurd. First, there was what she had already realized: that Rodney would never have been a party to the Mrs Belcher episode, and second, the scheme was unnecessarily complicated. If either or both had wished to murder Maurice, they could have done it without all this elaboration.

Her mind reverted to George's illness. Innocent or guilty, it was certainly a strange coincidence that it should have occurred on the very night of the murder. Of course he had had two or three earlier attacks. But still – Did it not almost look like design?

Her heart gave a leap as she thought, was it part of a design? It was genuine of course in the sense of real, but was it natural? Had it been purposely brought about? Had George deliberately eaten something indigestible or perhaps taken a minute dose of poison?

There was no reason to suppose so, but now Pauline's imagination was aflame. Those earlier attacks? Could they have been experimental to determine the amount of the dose? As she thought of just how bad they had been, she felt this might well be the truth.

Then she had a revulsion of feeling. Her fears were groundless. George would never have gone out in the early morning. He wouldn't have risked her waking and missing him.

But would he not? Could he not in fact have gone out without any risk? Once again sick from apprehension, she saw very clearly how he could have done so.

Some short time earlier she had been troubled by sleeplessness and Dr Manning had given her tablets to be taken when required at her discretion. She had not used all of these and the bottle was in the medicine cupboard in the bathroom.

Then flashed into her mind her awakening that morning. She was normally an early riser, but on this occasion she had slept for over an hour longer than usual. Also when she wakened she was feeling tired and unrested. She had supposed that these phenomena were the result of her late night. But now she remembered that on many occasions she had been up till later than one and had never overslept in consequence. Her tired and unrested feeling, moreover, was exactly what she had always experienced after taking the tablets.

With a dreadful excitement rising in her mind she sat trying to recall how many tablets there were in the bottle. The dose was two, and the bottle had contained twelve tablets for six doses. She had taken two doses – four tablets – so there ought to be eight left. She went again and again over the circumstances and became absolutely convinced that her recollection was correct.

For some time she fought her desire to examine the bottle. George after all was her husband, and though she had cause to doubt his fidelity, to suspect him of murder was a very different matter. But she presently found that she could no longer bear the uncertainty. George was dining in Radbury and she was alone in the house. She went to the bathroom and emptied the tablets out on to the table. There were six.

So two tablets had disappeared! She stood rigid, wondering could she by any chance have made a mistake as to the number she had taken. But she knew she hadn't. Someone else had unquestionably taken two tablets.

She felt stunned. There could no longer be any doubt. George had doped her. And if so had he not poisoned himself? For what?

As she stood there motionless beside the table a slight sound penetrated into her consciousness. Startled, she glanced up. George was standing at the door. He was watching her with a curious intentness. His questioning eyes searched her face. Then they left it and dropped to the table. She could see him noting the bottle and counting the six tiny discs which lay beside it. As he did so his expression changed subtly. Incredulity, dismay, dread and indecision chased themselves in turn across his features.

"Hullo," he said, and his voice was thick and he swayed slightly. "Not more insomnia, I hope?"

Pauline stared at him. She simply could not speak. "Well?" he went on more sharply, "what's taken you? You look as if you'd seen a ghost." Now she got the reek of whisky from his breath.

She was afraid of him in this state, not exactly drunk yet not wholly sober. While his normal self-control seemed weakened, his mental reactions remained acute, if slower in action. She doubted whether she could deceive him.

Indeed she did not try. An overwhelming urge seized her. In one way or another she must end this nightmare. Impulsively she cried out: "There are two missing! You took them, George! You gave them to me – in the tea – that night!"

Something like horror now showed on his face. For a moment they stood motionless, gazing at one another. Then his expression changed. She saw his features harden into a dreadful look of hate. He shrugged heavily.

"What's taken you, Pauline? Have you gone out of your mind? How can you say such a thing?"

"You know it!" she panted. "You drugged me! Why? What did you do that night that I mustn't know?"

He made a gesture as if to calm her. "My dear girl, you've gone dotty. I neither drugged you nor did anything that night. What's upset you so?"

For a moment she wondered could he be speaking the truth, then the look in his eyes told her. It told her more. It told her that he was capable of doing her an injury. A sudden panic seized her. Surely, oh surely, she couldn't be in personal danger? They were alone in the house and he was between her and the door. She could not get out if she wanted to.

Bitterly she regretted her outburst as she wondered how she could undo the mischief. Half crying, she forced herself to murmur, "Yes, I'm silly. It's this ghastly business going on and on and on. These police! Forget it, George. I'll be better presently."

He seemed relieved. "I tell you what you want," he said, "and I want it too. Whisky. That'll put us both right. Go into the lounge and I'll get it."

He spoke so quietly that she began to feel she had been a fool. She had let her imagination run away with her. It was what she had said: the strain of these last days. "Oh do, George," she agreed. "I've all gone to pieces. A drink will pull me together."

She went into the lounge and he followed to the hall. She heard him moving about in the dining-room. Then came the clink of glasses and presently the rush from the soda siphon. She sat down at the fire. Was she mad, or had George really been out in the small hours of that awful night? Common sense told her that what she imagined could not be the truth, yet where had the tablets gone? And why was George's manner so terrifying? She felt completely up against it. Situated as she was there was no one, literally *no one*, in whom she could confide. Rodney she usually went to with her difficulties, but she dared not do so this time. If it had been an outside affair she might have consulted Major Harwood, who she imagined was fond of Anne and therefore would be sympathetic to any member of the family. But now the very thought of applying to him made her hysterical. She felt –

Suddenly her thoughts swung back to the present. Was it not a long time since she had heard the soda going in? What could George be doing? She listened a little breathlessly.

What was that? A soft click coming, not from the dining-room, but from George's study. It was like the opening of his cupboard, a locked receptacle on the wall where he kept his special medicines for the animals, and other odds and ends. She stood up silently and tiptoed to the door. There was a mirror in the hall which from where she was standing reflected the study. But the study door was nearly closed and obstructed her view. Silently, her heart in her mouth, she pushed it slightly further open. Then, by manoeuvring, she was able to see the cupboard. She was able to see George and what he was doing.

She had read of people's blood running cold, but she had never believed that such a thing actually occurred. Now she knew. It seemed to her that for the first time she felt horror:

that which she had experienced earlier was but a pale shadow of the real thing. On the table before George was a glass of yellow liquid, no doubt the whisky and soda. He was just putting into the cupboard a small white bottle. She recognized that bottle. It contained prussic acid, which he had got during the previous summer to destroy wasps' nests.

For a moment Pauline could not believe the evidence of her eyes. Then the hideous truth forced itself into her consciousness. There could be no doubt what was in his mind. He would bring in two glasses. One would be safe. She knew which she would drink.

At first she felt absolutely paralysed, unable to move. Then a panic urge to be out of the house seized her. But now it was too late. George had replaced the bottle and with the glass in his hand was moving towards the hall. He must not see her. She shrank back into the lounge. Escape was barred. He was outside the door.

In desperation her eyes swung to the windows. There was no help in them. They were old-fashioned and stiff, and before she could open one he would be there. No, physically there was no escape. Her only hope lay in her wits. If she could not outwit him, she was finished.

She could hear him putting the glasses on a tray. He would be in directly: seconds only were left to her. Then, just as she heard his approaching step, an idea flashed into her mind. Swinging round, she seized the tongs, picked up a hot coal from the fire and flung it against the wall behind the sofa. She had just time to put down the tongs and crouch before the fire when he entered.

As she expected, there were two glasses on the tray, a small round one of enamelled plastic. He put it down carefully so that one glass should be opposite each of them.

She rose unsteadily and picked up hers. "This is what I want," she made herself say, but her voice sounded hoarse and strange. Then she glanced over his shoulder towards the sofa. She made herself stare fixedly and look surprised. Still staring, she put down her glass again on the tray.

"Smoke, George!" she shouted urgently, pointing behind him. "The place must be on fire!"

He swung round as she had hoped, and as he did so she took her chance and rotated the tray through a half circle. He did not appear to notice. Instantly she ran to the sofa.

"My fault," she declared bitterly. "I lit a cigarette as I went over to get a handkerchief I'd left there and I must have dropped the match. I wasn't thinking of what I was doing."

As she spoke she worked. The coal had rolled against the sofa valance and this was now on fire. With her foot she pushed the coal out of sight where it would do little harm on the hardwood floor, and began beating at the flames. He joined her and they quickly had them out. Pauline began to cry.

"Is there no end?" she sobbed brokenly. "One thing after another! I feel like committing suicide, I'm so fed up. Lord, I want that drink!"

She went back to the table and picked up her glass, the one which had been George's. Now was the crucial moment! Her hope was to prevent him suspecting she knew his purpose. If she could do this he wouldn't think about the glasses. But the least doubt in his mind and it would be the end. And it wouldn't be enough if she avoided the poison. If she were to escape with her life he must drink it. Could she make him?

She put all her strength into a last despairing effort. Holding out her glass towards him, she gasped, "Here, let us drink to an end of unhappiness and misunderstanding." Clink!

Almost to her surprise he followed her across the room, staggering slightly. Scarcely daring to breathe, she stood waiting. Then she came near to collapsing from relief. He picked up his glass, clinked it against hers, and they both drank.

Instantly his face changed. It took on a look of baffled fury. He made as if to hurl the glass at her, but his strength went and he collapsed in a heap on the floor.

For a moment Pauline stood looking at him, then her strength went too and she fell back helpless into a chair. She fought an insane desire to laugh, to laugh and laugh till the tears rolled down her cheeks. But the whisky she had drunk steadied her. Instinctively she got up and staggered to the kitchen, to be rid of that awful silent presence. Sitting down before the stove, she tried to rally her thoughts.

It was some time before she could think at all, and when at last she did so it was only to feel her sanity slipping from her. Slowly she began to realize her position. She had murdered her husband! It was true that she had acted in self-defence. That might have a bearing on her guilt, but it did not affect the fact. She, Pauline Selmer, was a murderess. She was now a marked woman. Never again could she get rid of the stain. Never again could life be the same.

Then a numbing fear gripped her. Had she not exchanged one danger for another? Who would believe her story? Would French, with his inexorable mind, probing into the dark springs of human action? George had been running after other women, he had been drinking, his temper had been vile, in fact, her position as his wife had been impossible. Who would believe that he had tried to kill her? Would not all the evidence point to her as the aggressor?

The burden she felt overwhelming, too great for her to carry alone. She must have human sympathy and help. There must be someone she could trust and to whom she could go for aid. But whom? Despairingly she went over in her mind the list of her friends.

Rodney of course was the one to whom she would naturally turn. But here doubts again assailed her. Suppose, however unlikely it might be, that Rodney himself was involved? Would he then help her? Or, incredibly, would he also be an enemy? Should she go instead to Rupert? Since the tragedy he had been much kinder and more approachable. He would certainly do what he could.

Then she had a revulsion of feeling. Here again were her wicked doubts. Rodney would never be an enemy. He had always been good to her and he would not fail her now. Besides, in the dreadful position he was in she must show her faith in him. He would be terribly hurt if she passed him by.

Fear had sharpened her wits. Should she leave the lights on in the house or turn them out? The Bungalow was out of sight from the main road, but someone passing along one of the footpaths might notice the windows. And their evidence must support whatever tale she afterwards told.

Presently she decided to leave the lights as they were. Then she slipped silently out of the back door, which was in darkness, and set off to the House.

It was another night like that on which she had walked over to attend Rodney's meeting, the apparent start of all their troubles. But on this occasion there was a damp fog over the sea, and at intervals the melancholy moaning of horns came to her as ships nosed their way up or down

Channel. It might be well to keep her visit secret, but the possibility of this would depend on where Rodney happened to be. When she reached the House, therefore, she turned to the left and followed the wall till she came to his sitting room at the side overlooking the terrace. The windows were lighted up. She crept up to one and tapped gently.

At first nothing happened and she tapped again. Then the curtain was pushed aside and Rodney looked out. She shook her head and put her finger on her lips. Rodney pulled the curtain further aside and softly opened the window.

"Let me come in," she whispered. "I must speak to you secretly."

The windows were high above the ground, and the sill was level with her shoulders. Rodney leaned out, put his arms beneath hers and lifted, while she pulled herself up by gripping the sill. In a few seconds she was in the room. Rodney closed window and curtain and looked at her keenly.

"You're in trouble," he declared. "Come and sit down and have a drink."

She relaxed thankfully before the fire while sipping the whisky he had poured out. Then the horror of her position once more swept over her.

"Oh, Rodney," she muttered, half whispering, half crying, "something awful has happened! Something too ghastly to speak of. I don't know how to tell you. It's George!"

"George?" Rodney spoke sharply but in a low tone. "Has he been misconducting himself? If he's made himself a nuisance I'll give him the hiding of his life!"

She wrung her hands. "Oh, don't speak like that," she moaned. "He's – he's – dead! He must be!"

Rodney's jaw dropped. "Good God! Dead! You can't mean it, Pauline?"

She nodded despairingly. "It's true, Rodney, it's true. And worse than that! I killed him!"

"Pauline, don't say it. I can't believe it. What happened?"

Stammering and with hesitations she told him everything that she had done and thought, save only her fears of his own guilt. She could see that he was deeply moved.

"You poor thing," he said when she had finished. "It's a ghastly mix-up. I'm glad you came straight to me."

"I couldn't carry on alone and I knew you'd help me. What can it all mean?"

"Never mind that now: time for it later. We must see first what's to be done."

"Yes, that's right. But, Rodney, I'm afraid it's still worse than I told you. I've been asking myself, who will believe my story? Will French, because he's the one who matters?"

Rodney gestured vehemently. "My dear, get such an idea out of your head! You mean that you might be suspected? What rubbish! What absolute nonsense! No one could suspect you."

"But couldn't they? Look here, Rodney, you may not have known it, but George had gone off the rails lately. I hate to speak evil of him as things are, but the truth is necessary. George recently has been unfaithful to me. He's been running after some woman in Bristol."

"I didn't know. I'm sorry."

"He's been drinking, particularly since Maurice – went, and his temper has been simply vile. It hasn't been very easy lately, I can tell you. And he had made a will in my favour. I had plenty of motive."

He shook his head. "That's simply morbid. You must put away such thoughts."

"No, it's not and I mustn't. It's true, Rodney. French will find all that out and then what will he think?"

"Nobody could believe you guilty," Rodney declared, but his tone had lost conviction. "Have another drink while I think it over."

She did not want more whisky, but kept silence so as not to interrupt the flow of his thought. Oh, what a relief it had been to come up and share the ghastly news! Rodney was going to help her. And there was no one, *no one*, more competent to do so. The situation would indeed be black from which Rodney could not find a way out.

For some minutes he remained silent, then he turned to her and there was a new purpose and decision in his manner. "Now look here, Pauline, we'll fix this up, but you must help. You must do exactly what I tell you. Your own safety may depend on it. Understand?"

To be taken in charge and told what to do was of all things what she wanted. "Of course, Rodney. Whatever you say."

"Good. Now you must get out of the window again and go round and knock at the front door. Fortunately you put on the sort of wrap you'd wear if you were coming to see the pater. Ask for him, and say you were free for the moment and came up to see how he was. Follow?"

She nodded.

"Go up and see him. He's rather better tonight and he'll enjoy talking to you. Don't volunteer it, but somehow convey to him that you're worried about George, and that you really came up because he arrived home drunk. Say you want him to be asleep before you go back."

"That seems dreadful, Rodney."

"You can't help it. I needn't hide from you a mistake now might land you in some danger. To do what I say is your best chance. Besides it's the truth. You'll tell the pater?"

"Very well, if I get an opportunity."

"No, that's no good. You must make your opportunity. I tell you, this is vital."

"All right, Rodney. I'll do it."

"Try and keep him interested for at least half an hour. Then say you'll look in on me on your way home and come down here. I may not be here, and if not, wait for me. I'll arrive presently by the window. Now are you clear about all that?"

"Perfectly. What are you going to do?"

"Nothing that interests you. You don't know a thing about my movements. If the question arises, you'll say you found me here when you came in and that we just sat chatting."

"Oh, Rodney, what a comfort you are! I was at the end of my tether."

"With luck we'll pull it off. Now don't lose any more time."

He helped her out of the window and she went round to the front door. There she stood for some seconds, fighting for coolness and her usual bearing. Finally setting her teeth, she rang.

It all proved easier than she had expected. She found herself able to speak quite normally to Lamson, and when she had given him her wraps and gone upstairs, she was positive that he had noticed nothing unusual. So it was with Sir Leigh. He was obviously glad to see her and talked of his own affairs without looking at her closely. But Nurse M'Candless was different. Very observant and anything but a fool, Pauline felt that she could not deceive her if once her suspicions were aroused. Fortunately after a few seconds the nurse took herself off.

Pauline sat down and listened to the old man's rambling monotone. He had gone to pieces terribly since Maurice's death and it was clear that the end was not far off. Dreadful as it was to see him in such a state, tonight she was thankful for it. With his eyes half closed he was talking about his youth. A word or two at intervals was all she had to supply. She could just about do it and no more. All the same she did manage to give him the information about George.

Presently he grew tired. She glanced at the clock. She had been with him for the required half-hour. She therefore got up and said good night to him. As she went out she knocked at the nurse's door.

"I think I've been there long enough," she said. "He's getting sleepy; I'll just look in on the Brigadier on my way out."

It was rather dark in the passage and she stood with her back to the light. The nurse bid her good night, obviously having noticed nothing. Pauline went downstairs, tapped at Rodney's door and went in, closing the door behind her.

The room was empty, but the curtains across the window were swaying. She peeped behind them. The window was open. Fortunately it was a calm night. The movement had been due, not to wind, but to the closing of the door.

She sat down at the fire and gave herself up to thought. How disasters came together! Her life had gone on for years, not exactly uneventfully, but in an ordinary and on the whole a happy way, and now look what had happened! Her marriage spoilt by George's infatuation for that woman, Sir Leigh's illness, Maurice's murder, the police inquiry, and now this ghastly crowning horror. How would it end? Her arrest? Rodney's arrest? She just couldn't bear to follow it any further.

What, she wondered, could Rodney be doing? She supposed he had gone to the Bungalow, but what action he could take when he got there she could not imagine. Uneasily she reminded herself that she had not examined George before leaving. She had known she ought to do so, but she just couldn't bring herself to go back into that room. Not, she told herself, that there was any chance of his being alive. During her nursing she had picked up some knowledge of hydrocyanic acid. It paralysed the heart and lungs, often within seconds of smelling or taking it. Death usually occurred within minutes. When a person had been paralysed by it, as George had been, there was no hope that he would live.

Her thoughts swung round to French. What would he think about George? What...

A shuffling attracted her attention. The curtains moved aside and Rodney dropped lightly into the room. "Everything all right with you?" he asked. "No suspicions aroused?"

"No, I'm sure there weren't. Everything went normally. What about you?"

He closed the window softly and sat down beside her at the fire. "I think I've fixed it," and for a moment he looked old and worn. "Let me tell you what you're to know. There may not be much time, so listen carefully."

"Go on, Rodney. I'm listening."

"When George came in this evening he was, not exactly drunk, but as they say, under the influence. He was bad-tempered, noisy and quarrelsome."

"He was partly drunk, but not noisy."

"He was noisy and quarrelsome. Don't forget that. The details of his coming in you can take from real life. Tell the police just what happened. But he was noisy and quarrelsome and you became afraid of a scene."

"Yes, I see what you're getting at."

"You'll have to decide in your own mind whether you were or were not afraid of violence. I should say better not. You were afraid of an unpleasant scene. You therefore decided to come up here for an hour or two till George should go to bed. Once he was asleep, as he soon would be, there should be no fear of trouble, because in the morning he would be repentant, as he always was. Is that quite clear?"

"Yes, perfectly."

"Very well, that's all you have to know. You of course know nothing of any attempt to murder you. There was no fire under the sofa. You had no drinks in the lounge. When you discovered the condition he was in you simply slipped away, and that's all you know."

"I follow you, Rodney, but what have you done?"

"That's all you know," he repeated. "Stick to that and don't embellish and you'll be all right."

She shivered. "Oh, Rodney, I wish it was true! I hate the lying."

"So do I, Pauline. But I've thought it out. It's the only way."

"I'm not questioning it and I'll do it. What should I have done if you hadn't helped me?"

"My dear girl, it's not over yet. You won't find the police questioning easy. But stick to your story and, again, don't embellish. If they ask you anything not covered by your story, you just don't know."

"I understand." Then she went on hesitatingly, "Tell me, did you see him? He was..."

"He was dead, but you shouldn't know that either."

They went on talking desultorily, then Pauline started. "That's surely the Radbury fire horn?" she asked.

"Sounds like it. Some outbreak in the town probably."

Five minutes later the telephone rang. They heard Lamson's quiet voice, then an exclamation, then hurried steps and the door was thrown open. The old man looked white and shaken.

"The Bungalow, sir! The Bungalow! It's on fire!"

– 9 –

THE AFTERMATH OF FIRE

When French and Carter received Bowman's message they at once got out their car and followed him to the fire. It was damp and foggy and very dark and they could not make much speed. When they turned into the Bungalow drive a dull flickering glow appeared in the sky, which quickly brightened as they got closer, finally resolving itself into the burning house. It showed up as a white hot interior from which great tongues of flame belched from the windows and roof.

They parked under the trees along the drive, leaving the area in front of the house clear for the firemen. Two engines had arrived and were clacking industriously. Fortunately there was a small pond close by and hoses had been run into it. Powerful jets of water were already hissing into the incandescent mass.

At first it had seemed as if the whole house were ablaze, but on approaching nearer they saw that only one end was involved. The bedrooms were already practically gutted and the roof over them had partially collapsed, but the other end containing the sitting rooms was so far intact though smoking.

As they reached Bowman, who was standing with the chief of the fire brigade, three running figures appeared.

French recognized them as Rupert and Rodney Vale and Pauline. They rushed up to Bowman, shouting and gesticulating.

"My husband!" Pauline screamed. "Has he been got out? He was there, in the house!" While Rodney cried: "Mr Selmer! Mr Selmer! Has anyone seen him? Is he safe?"

Two firemen had just put on oxygen masks, and these now hurried forward. They quickly broke the glass of one of the lounge windows and disappeared into the smoke. A rapid inquiry among the spectators showed that no one had seen George.

Time seemed to pause while the jets hissed and the flames roared upwards, throwing coruscations of sparks into the dark sky. Then two more masked firemen appeared and followed the others.

Again time lagged, but at length all four reappeared. Quickly they made their report. There was no one in the lounge or other two sitting-rooms on that side of the hall, nor, so far as could be seen, in the hall itself. The hall was not actually burning, but flames were shooting into it from the bedrooms and kitchen in the other wing. It would be a matter of seconds only till it was alight. The bedroom wing was an absolute inferno and no one in it could be alive.

French turned to the brothers. "Take Mrs Selmer away, gentlemen. She can do nothing, and waiting here will only harrow her feelings unnecessarily."

"She won't come. She means to wait till she knows."

"If the flames were out now, it still wouldn't be possible to enter those bedrooms for several hours. We won't know till the morning. Get her away as soon as you can."

The blazing end of the bungalow being obviously beyond help, the firemen were concentrating on saving the sitting-rooms. At last it became clear that they had prevented the flames from crossing the hall. Then they turned their jets on to the burning rooms and slowly the fire died down. In an hour only smoke was pouring from the wreck.

French approached Bowman. "What do you think of this, Super? Any ideas?"

"How do you mean, any ideas?"

"No notion of how the place got alight, I suppose?"

Bowman shook his head. "I've only got one pointer and it's by no means conclusive. I'm informed the wing went up very quickly."

"Yes?"

"The man who gave the alarm was passing along the footpath from the railway when he saw it. The windows of only one room were then lighted up, and he would have thought it was just that the room was occupied only that the light was flickering. He hurried over to make sure, but before he reached the house one of the curtains went up in a blaze. He rushed to the door and banged with the knocker. There was no reply, and as he couldn't open the door, he ran to the nearest house and rang up the brigade. He went back to the bungalow and the whole wing was then ablaze. He said he couldn't have believed the fire would spread so quickly."

"As you say, that might mean something or it might not. But Mr Selmer seems to have disappeared. A bit of a coincidence coming so soon after the other affair. Makes you think, or doesn't it?"

"I've been thinking ever since I came out. But we won't know till we're able to examine those rooms."

"Should we take any precautions?"

"Such as?"

"Well, what about putting on some men to see that no one goes near the place?"

"I agree. Matter of fact I'd already decided on it."

They discussed the possibility of examination with the chief of the brigade, and there being no chance of doing anything that night, they set their guard and returned to Radbury. The Vale brothers and Pauline had disappeared some time earlier.

When French and Carter reached the station next morning they found that a message had just come in from the Bungalow. It was believed that the rooms were now cool enough to enter.

"You'd better not go like that, French, unless you want to spoil a good suit of clothes," Bowman remarked. He himself was got up in a particularly grimy boiler suit. "There's a spare one of these if you'd like it."

French thanked him and drew on the suit. As he was doing so the chief of the fire brigade arrived. "Meet Mr Haines, French," Bowman introduced. "He's coming out to have a pow-wow over this affair."

Haines was a big burly man with a particularly shrewd eye. "How are you, Mr French? I didn't like the look of things out there and I thought we'd better go through the place together."

"Very glad of your advice, Mr Haines. The Super and I were both wondering if everything was just what it seemed. Nothing more has been learned?"

"No one has entered the house. Your men wouldn't allow it and I think they were right. We'll be sure that nothing's been disturbed."

French was interested to see that Bowman was bringing with him not only his photographer, but also his fingerprint man. It showed the direction of his thoughts.

They drove out almost in silence, dismounting on the gravel before the house. There are few more tragic and woebegone sights than that of a recently burnt-out building, and this one was no exception to the rule. One end was completely gutted. The roof was gone and the walls stood up stark and blackened round the charred debris within. The hall remained, a hideous chaos of half-burnt furniture, peeling walls and pools of foul water. But except for the wet and dirt over everything, the sitting-room end had escaped.

The men's first care was to see if there was any trace of George in the building. A quick glance showed that the firemen had been correct in saying there was none in either sitting-rooms or hall, and they stepped carefully into the burnt-out wing. It was not long before they found his body.

The tiles from the roof had partially covered everything, but had not moved objects sideways, and it was possible to reconstruct the position before the fire. George had obviously been lying on a bed, of which only the metal frame was left. Close beside it was the wreck of an electric fire. Broken glass was there too, and French saw quickly that it would have built up into a decanter and tumbler. The body was dreadfully burnt, but not wholly destroyed.

"Lay down on the bed with the whisky, having moved the electric fire too close to the bedclothes, then fell asleep," Bowman remarked. "At least that's the obvious conclusion."

"Could be," French agreed. Then he grinned. "I'm afraid, Super, you're of a suspicious turn of mind."

"Aren't you?"

"I admit it with regret. All the same, we've nothing to go on except the unlikelihood of these two tragedies being unconnected."

"Isn't that plenty?"

"I suppose it is. Well, let's have a look round and then we'll hear Mrs Selmer's story."

"Which won't help much, if I'm any judge." French thought of an admirable retort, then decided it would be impolitic. They sent a man to telephone for Dr Manning and an ambulance, and had photographs taken of the body and its surroundings. French wandered about, but he saw nothing that interested him except in the lounge. There, part of the sofa was burnt and a coal had fallen on the hardwood floor, charring the blocks. To this he called Bowman's attention.

"What price that for attempted arson?" the Super said triumphantly.

"So you'd say at first sight," French admitted. "But what put it out? That valance had caught properly and the fire would certainly have spread to the whole room. Why didn't it?"

"You may have something there. See what Mrs Selmer says."

By the time French had finished his inspection Dr Manning arrived. "What's this?" he grunted. "They tell me Selmer's dead?"

"A body's in there," Bowman nodded. "We think it's Selmer's."

"Hard luck on the family. And so soon after that other." The doctor looked in through the window opening. "Man alive, you don't expect me to crawl about in that dirty hole? Have the body lifted out."

"What about seeing it before it's moved, Doctor?" Bowman grinned.

Manning glanced again through the window. "I've seen it," he declared. "You have photographs, no doubt?"

"Yes, we never scamp our duty."

"Oh, you don't, don't you? I'll remember that one."

The body was lifted on to the stretcher and carried out. Dr Manning bent over it. Then he called Bowman.

"Any ideas about this affair, Super?" he asked, transfixing the other with a shrewd eye and unconsciously repeating French.

"Ideas?" Bowman returned innocently. "No, Doctor, I was hoping to get them from you."

"Well, if you haven't been using your head up till now, you'll soon have to start. Those burns were received after death."

"They were? Now that interests me quite a bit. You hear that, French?"

"We were just talking about it," said French calmly. "We thought it might be so. And that, Doctor, leads up to…?"

Manning simulated wrath. "Quite: put it on me. You and Bowman! Birds of a feather! Well, French, I can't tell you without a p-m. Get me the order, Bowman, and I'll push on with it as quickly as I can."

"Right, Doctor. You'll have it without delay."

"A good chap," said French as Manning drove off. "One of the best. He'll do everything he can to help us. And a first-rate doctor too. What are you going to do next, French?"

"Is this my job?"

"Well, what do you think? I imagined we'd agreed it was connected with the other."

"So we had, and this from the doctor supports the idea. All right, suits me. If I'm messing about here I can't be working at the Yard. There are compensations to everything."

"Well, I'll leave you to it. Anything you want me to do?"

"Not at the moment. I'll call on Mrs Selmer first. A lot will depend on her story."

"You've said it. Right then, see you later." He waved his hand and drove off.

"Willing they all are, Carter, to let us carry the baby. I suppose since they've hired a dog, they don't see why they should do the barking."

"They don't know what barking to do, if you ask me, sir. It's a proper tangle anyhow."

"How right you are. Well, that seems to finish us here. Let's go and see that woman."

They drove to the House and French asked for Pauline.

"She's lying down, sir," Lamson replied, and he looked as if a day or two in bed wouldn't hurt him either. "I'll send Susan up to tell her you're here."

"Say I'm sorry to trouble her, but she knows herself how urgent the matter is."

Lamson showed them into the library and presently Pauline came down. She looked pale and tired, which, French felt, was natural. But he was at once interested by her manner. She was, he was certain, not merely nervous. She was frightened. Indeed he thought she was terrified. Once again it was borne in on him that she knew more – now he thought a lot more – than she admitted. He expressed regret for troubling her, offered a guarded sympathy, and suggested that she must be as anxious as he was to know what had taken place.

"Of course, Mr French," she answered, "please don't think it necessary to apologize. We'll all be glad of your help in clearing up this awful affair."

"Very good of you to say so, madam. Strictly speaking it's not my business, but Mr Bowman had an appointment and asked me to act for him." If this was not strictly true, French felt the deviation was in a good cause. "Perhaps you will kindly tell me what you can about last evening?"

"Certainly." Pauline repeated her story with, she believed, credit. George had come in about nine, having dined with some friends in Radbury. She had at once seen that he was the worse for drink. No, not exactly drunk, but excited and quarrelsome. Yes, it had happened before, but not often. She would not say that he had formed the habit of drinking, but occasionally he did take a little too much, particularly if he dined out. As she said, he was quarrelsome, and he began to abuse her for not letting him invite his friends to dine at his home instead of having to take them to a Radbury hotel. Well, yes, there was something in his grievance. She was only too glad to see his personal friends, but not mere business acquaintances. This Mr Hobson and his partner Mr Cadnam were only that. She had no help with the cooking and she didn't see why she should have extra work on their account. However, she supposed these details would not interest Mr French: all she meant was that George thought she was to blame and began to abuse her. She therefore told him she would go for a time to Cheddon House and she at once did so. She intended to stay there till he had gone to bed, as she knew he would do early, and he always fell asleep at once. In the morning he would be normal and repentant for any trouble he had given her. She came up to the House, saw Sir Leigh, and was sitting chatting to Rodney when someone telephoned about the fire.

French made a show of accepting this story at its face value, and as it progressed he was interested to see Pauline's fear slowly diminish and her self-confidence return. Was this due to relief that she had successfully put something over? He could not explain it otherwise.

"Thank you, Mrs Selmer, that's all very clear," he told her. "There's just one other point; I don't know if you can tell me anything about it. There seems to have been a second fire at the Bungalow. I noticed that the lounge sofa had been alight. Do you know anything with regard to that?"

Once again fear shone in her eyes, but she answered collectedly enough. "Oh yes, that also happened last night. George lit a cigarette and absently threw the match behind the sofa instead of into the fire. It must have lodged in the valance, for that blazed up. But George beat it out at once."

So she was lying! It was impossible not to believe that the fire had been caused by the hot coal which had scorched the floor beneath the valance. She could have denied all knowledge of the affair and French might not have been able to shake her statement, but this was a give-away. For a moment he considered taxing her with the deception, then he thought it would be better to wait until he knew more. He got up, thanked her again, and he and Carter took their leave.

"Back to Radbury," he growled as they reached the car.

It was not till after lunch that Dr Manning's report on the p-m was received. George had died from a large dose of prussic acid, probably taken in whisky. Though French had realized the possibility of foul play, he was not prepared for this. It of course altered his whole outlook on the affair, making George's death as important as Maurice's.

Accident, suicide or murder? Long and painful experience had taught French the value of system. Accident? With such a poison, so improbable that he need not consider it. Suicide? From all he had known of George, and indeed from Pauline's recent statement, he might dismiss this also. That left murder.

There seemed to be two promising lines of approach. Who could have desired George's death and who could have brought it about? French was rather horrified at the speed and certainty with which the answers came. George had been a drunken and ill-tempered husband, for it was likely that Pauline's statement had minimized conditions. A comparatively young woman tied to such a man, and possibly knowing someone else with whom she could be happy, would have a motive. And who better than that wife, according to her own statement alone with her husband at the critical time, could have given him the dose?

When, presently, he saw Bowman, French found that the Super's thoughts had been travelling in the same direction as his own, but Bowman had made a reservation. "The thing that sticks me, French, is the lady's character. I don't know her very well, of course, but she has a certain reputation. I admit it's not conclusive, but I just can't think of her doing such a thing. All the same I'd lay any odds she knows something about it."

"I agree. Well, Super, I suppose there's nothing for it but another look over the house. We've got to find the prussic acid for one thing."

"Right. I'll be here if you want anything."

French and Carter drove again to the Bungalow. There French began one of those exhaustive searches which murder cases invariably involve. First he looked once again at the sofa. The floor showed slight scorching under where the burnt valance had hung and deeper marks further under the sofa. On these last the cinder was still lying. There could be no doubt that a live coal from the fire had been dropped at the first place, that it had there set the valance alight, and that either deliberately or in the beating out of the fire, it had been pushed to where it now lay. It was quite impossible that the story of the cigarette match should be true.

French moved on to George's study. Here his search was quickly rewarded. In a cupboard, the lock of which he had to pick, was a half-empty bottle of potassium cyanide. It bore the label of a Radbury chemist, but no fingerprints.

Could George, fuddled and in a fit of temporary despondency through drink, have poured poison into a glass of whisky and taken it with him to bed? French did not think so. If he had been going to take the stuff, he would have done it there at the cupboard. It was not as if it acted slowly like an overdose of a sleeping draught: insensibility came within seconds.

But if he had gone to bed and clamoured for a drink, nothing would have been easier than for Pauline to take him one and to dope it before she did so. She could then have arranged the fire in the hope of destroying all damaging evidence. She could have put the electric heater close to the bed to account for the outbreak. Of course French had learned enough to see that it did not do so. The length of time between her arrival and the outbreak of the fire postulated some delayed action apparatus. She would indeed have employed such for her own sake. Further, the speed with which the fire spread, once it had started, suggested artificial stimulus. Probably petrol or paraffin had been poured about the room.

It was obvious that Pauline could have done all this, but if it was improbable that she would commit a simple murder, it was still less likely that she could be guilty of such a hideous crime as this. French saw that he must confront her with the inconsistencies of her statement. But first he must complete certain other inquiries.

Some of George's papers were in the desk in his study and some in his office in the farmyard. French went through both lots with care. With one exception he found only what he expected to find: bills, cancelled cheques, correspondence, accounts and the like, none of which interested him. But the exception made up for the dullness of the rest. In a drawer of the small safe which housed George's most important documents was a single sheet of quarto White Bank typing paper bearing the following typewritten words:

> Modelling clay, putty or plasticine will do, but plasticine is the handiest. Rapid setting cement reinforced with wire is best for the other.
>
> A R

French stared in amazement, then slowly gave vent to a lurid oath. The words were puzzling enough, but what thrilled him was not the words, but the typescript. It was that of the other vital letters in the case, the one about Molly Crawford's alleged discovery that Cheddon hid a secret, and the other which had brought Maurice out to his death.

French examined the paper more carefully. It had evidently been picked up by someone with a dirty hand, for on the front lower corner was a clear thumb mark with the corresponding first finger mark on the back. George's, no doubt. Unhappily George's actual prints could no longer be taken, but French found numerous prints which must have been his in the safe and desk. They were different from those on the paper.

Here in this discovery was ample confirmation, had confirmation been needed, that George had been involved in the murder plot against Maurice. But what could the letter mean, for French supposed it was a letter? And who, he wondered, was "A R"? He looked through his book, but he had so far come across no one in the case with these initials. He sighed as it was borne in on him that he was even further from the solution than he had thought.

Then he told himself that it would be time enough to consider the affair later. He must continue work while it was daylight. They drove into Radbury and saw the chemist who had sold the potassium cyanide. Though the transaction had taken place several months earlier, when the man turned up his poison book he recalled the circumstances. George Selmer had bought the stuff for the alleged purpose of destroying wasps' nests. The purchase had been made perfectly openly.

French then went on to the office of Messrs Hobson and Cadnam, seed merchants, which was close by. There he was lucky enough to find Mr Hobson just about to leave for the night. After politenesses he turned back to his private room.

"I dare say, Mr Hobson," French went on, "you can guess why I have called. We're trying to find out the cause of the fire. Now my information is that when it broke out Mr Selmer was alone in the house; further, that he was somewhat under the influence of drink. You may be able to help me there. I understand you dined together that evening?"

Hobson nodded. "Yes, that's right. Selmer and Cadnam and I dined at the Grange Arms. It was really a business meeting. We discussed the supply of seeds and so on to the farm."

"Quite so, sir, but what I wanted to know was Mr Selmer's condition. Had he taken much alcohol?"

"We had drinks, of course, but not in any way to excess. We talked over our business perfectly normally and clearly. I can truthfully say that all three of us remained quite sober."

"After your business was done did Mr Selmer have one or two for the road?"

Hobson considered this. "That's right," he then conceded. "We all celebrated the agreement we had reached."

French was finding it hard to get what he wanted. "Did Mr Selmer take enough to affect him?" he asked bluntly.

At last Hobson admitted it. George was slightly fuddled when he left, and he would doubtless have been more so by the time he reached his home. But in Hobson's opinion he would have remained in complete control of himself, and he considered it absurd to suppose that he could accidentally have set the house on fire. All the same, Pauline's statement was so far exactly corroborated, and a further question showed that George had probably arrived home at about the time she said.

So much for Hobson. But further checking of Pauline's evidence was required, and the two men drove out once again to Cheddon House. First they saw Lamson. French explained that in order to try to find the hour of the outbreak, he wanted to know at what time Mrs Selmer had arrived, declaring that she herself was unable to remember.

Lamson was reassuringly clear on the point. It was about half past nine. He had noticed the time because he had listened to the nine o'clock news, and before her arrival had done jobs which would have taken him about fifteen minutes.

French went on to see Sir Leigh. Under the pretence of telling him how his researches into the Maurice affair were going, he obtained the old man's statement as to when Pauline had been with him on the fatal evening. His recollection probably was not too reliable, but Nurse

M'Candless, whom French next interviewed, confirmed the hours mentioned.

It seemed to French that nothing would be gained by a further delay in challenging Pauline. She was staying for the time being at the House, and he therefore told Lamson he wished to see her again. She presently joined Carter and him in the morning room, where there was a fire. French decided his best hope would be in a bluff.

"I'm sorry, Mrs Selmer," he said, speaking very gravely, "if this turns out to be an unpleasant interview, but if it does I can assure you that the fault is not mine, but yours. It is a mistake at all times to attempt to mislead the police, but when such takes the form of making a false statement in a murder case, the consequences are bound to be serious."

He paused and looked at her sternly. She had gone deadly pale, but she tried to take a high line. "Does all that mean that you are accusing me of lying to you?" she asked as frigidly as she could.

"It does, madam," French told her sharply, "and I'm now going to prove it to you." He decided that having made a good beginning, he should continue in the same strain. "But as it is impossible to say where this matter may end, before you say anything more it is my duty to tell you that you need not reply to my questions if you think your answers might incriminate you, and that before replying you are entitled to have your solicitor present."

She gazed at him in undisguised alarm. "Incriminate me?" she repeated weakly. "I don't know what you mean."

He shook his head. "Oh yes, you do, Mrs Selmer. Your husband has been murdered. On your own statement you were alone with him at the time. Your account of what took place between you is false. When I add to these points the fact that you had reason to wish for your freedom, you must see that I am justified."

French thought this had done it. He could see that she was overwhelmed with horror. In fact, she could not speak. He was sorry for her, as he had grown to like and respect her and he did not really believe her guilty. But he had to get his information and this seemed the only way.

"Look here, Mrs Selmer," he went on after he thought the silence had dragged on for long enough, "I am not your enemy. All I want is the truth. I am not at present accusing you of anything. You may be able to explain your action satisfactorily. But if you refuse to tell me what actually happened, what can I do but suspect the worst?"

He could see that a terrible struggle was going on in her mind. He believed he had said enough and that silence would now have most effect. He therefore waited. The minutes passed. As he expected, her tension continued to grow and at last, as he had hoped, she could bear it no longer. With a low moan she gave in. "Yes," she muttered, "what I said was not true. I don't know how you learned it, but you are right."

"Your story was contradicted by the evidence in the house, madam. I can't advise you, but if, remembering my caution, you decide to make a more correct statement, I can assure you it will be considered sympathetically."

Her hands were clasped until the knuckles showed white. "Oh," she cried brokenly, "I see I must speak! You've left me no option. It was ghastly! I can't tell you how ghastly it was! He tried – to kill me! And I – I – " she boggled at it, then with an immense effort got out, "I killed him! But it was in self-defence."

French saw that he had the truth at last. He could afford now to be generous. "If you can prove that, Mrs Selmer, you'll be all right. Now take it quietly and think of it as if you were speaking of someone other than yourself, and tell me exactly what occurred from beginning to end. Steady a moment," he added, holding up his hand. "Would you like a drink before you begin?"

She pointed to a cupboard. He went over, found whisky and a glass, and poured her out a stiff tot. It steadied her.

"Thank you," she said. "I wanted that."

"Now take it quite easily," he repeated. "Carter will note what you say, then he'll type it, and if you find it correct I shall ask you to sign it. That's all you'll have to do, at least for the present."

She seemed somewhat relieved. "I'll tell you everything," she said. "I happened to be thinking over the death of Mr Vale when a terrible idea shot into my mind," and she told him of how seriously George had taken the affair, how she had begun to wonder if he knew more about it than he had pretended, and how she had seen he could have left the house after she had fallen asleep, perhaps to carry the body to the railway. She told of the strange coincidence of his internal attack, and of her oversleeping next morning, culminating in her discovery of the missing sleeping tablets. She described how George had found her with the bottle, and admitted that she had lost her head and accused him of drugging her in order to do something secret during the night. She explained about the proposed drinks, and how she had heard him at his medicine cupboard, and seen in the mirror what he was doing. She recounted how in despair she had thrown the coal behind the sofa, and how when George turned to see the blaze she had reversed the glasses, ending up by saying she had decided to lie about all this in the hope that his death would be considered an accident.

That every word of this was the truth French had no doubt whatever. "That's better, Mrs Selmer," he told her. "I accept your statement unreservedly – as far as it has gone. But I think you have more to tell me."

Again she looked terrified. She shook her head weakly.

"Oh yes you have," French persisted. "For example, where did you leave the body?"

She shuddered. "I was to blame there too," she admitted in a strangled voice. "I didn't look to see – if he was dead. I felt sure he must be, but I couldn't bring myself to go back into that room."

"You mean Mr Selmer was lying on the floor in the lounge when you left the house?"

She seemed surprised. "Oh yes."

"And how did you suppose the fire had taken place?"

"I didn't understand that. I thought we couldn't have put out the sofa fire properly and that it had burned up again."

French shook his head. "It's no use, Mrs Selmer. I know your intention is good, but you're too honest to carry off a falsehood. Let me tell you two things. First, the fire broke out in the bedroom, and not till at least an hour after you left the house. Second, Mr Selmer's body was found on the bed in his room. Now who moved the body and who lit the fire?"

It was a knockout blow. She stared speechless and as if turned to stone.

"Let me make a suggestion," French went on. "You were naturally dreadfully upset and above everything you wanted help. You came up here and consulted either Major or Brigadier Vale or both. They went down and fixed things, though they didn't tell you how. Am I right?"

She still could not speak, but she was a child in French's hands, and presently she admitted that she had indeed appealed to Rodney. French saw that his next duty was to interrogate Rodney, but he was in doubt as to whether he should let Pauline see him first. He decided that this would be wise.

"Very well, Mrs Selmer, just one other question. Who was A R?"

She stared. "A R? I have no idea. Are they initials?"

"Yes. Don't you know who they refer to?"

She repeated that she had no idea, and he believed her. "Then," he told her, "that will be all at present. As soon as your statement is typed I shall ask you to check it over, and if correct, to sign it. We'll all want some dinner, but I'll come back afterwards to see Brigadier Vale."

"You've surprised me this time, sir," Carter remarked when they were outside. "I'd have thought you'd see the Brigadier at once."

"You might guess that, Carter. If we let her see Rodney she'll queer his pitch for him. If she tells him she's given him away, he can't very well hold out on us."

Carter was appreciative. "It's a fact, sir," he declared warmly. "She'll soften him up properly."

A couple of hours later they were back at Cheddon House. A glance at Rodney showed French that Pauline had done her job. Bluff was not likely to work as well with Rodney as with her, yet he thought a little might help.

"I'm sorry, sir, to have to remind you of what you know as well as I do," he began; "that keeping back information in a murder case is a serious matter and may lead to a charge of accessory after the fact."

Rodney was not to be caught with this. "If you're referring to what Mrs Selmer has just told you, as I presume you are," he returned, "that's where you're making your big mistake. I kept back no information about a murder. In point of fact no murder took place. Mrs Selmer killed her husband in self-defence as he was trying to kill her."

"You went down to the Bungalow and destroyed genuine evidence and substituted false. That made you an accessory after the fact. You set the Bungalow on fire to cover up what you had done. That may be arson. Whatever the circumstances of the death, you will have to meet those charges."

Rodney shrugged. "It may have been technically wrong," he admitted, "but morally I consider I did the right thing."

"I'm not here to judge that, sir, but to get the facts. I must give you a formal caution," and he did so. "Now after that if you will make a statement Carter will take it down and you can sign it later."

"I didn't intend to say anything about this," Rodney declared, "but I see I must. All right, I'll make the statement. About twenty past nine yesterday evening I was reading in my room when I heard a tap at the window." He went on to describe Pauline's visit and his own dismay at her position. Then he had suddenly seen a way in which the affair might be made to look like an accident. He had gone down to the Bungalow and found that George was dead. He had laid the body on George's bed and moved the electric fire near it, though not close enough to do any harm. He had carried up the decanter, soda siphon and a glass. He had found and lit four short candles, placing one on the bed and the others on various inflammable objects, so that when they burnt down at least one of them would set the house alight. He had found both petrol and paraffin and soaked the bed and other parts of the room. He had believed his scheme to be watertight and he didn't know how the Superintendent had seen through it. He declared he had no idea who A R was.

French was satisfied that once again he had been told the truth. "You underestimated the difficulty of a deception of that kind," he told Rodney, going on to repeat his demand for the signing of the statement when it should be typed.

Rodney seemed surprised. "Then," he asked a trifle shakily, "you're not going to charge me with these actions?"

French shook his head. "I'm not making any charge, though of course I can't answer for what may or may not be done in the future. You have answered my questions, which is all I want at present."

French felt that he should inform the Chief Constable of what he had learned. Having therefore left a note asking Bowman to arrange a conference, he returned to the hotel, weary after his long day.

– 10 –

"THE ADVENTURE OF THE PRIORY SCHOOL"

Next morning French was early at the police station. Bowman had just arrived and was actually reading his note as he entered the room.

"The CC had to go to London this morning," Bowman greeted him, "and won't be back for three or four days. What's turned up now?"

"Got admissions last night from two of those people at Cheddon House. You wouldn't have guessed it, Super, but it was Mrs Selmer who killed her husband."

Bowman stared.

"And Brigadier Rodney Vale, DSO, was an accessory after the fact," continued French. "He went down afterwards to the Bungalow to try and fake an accident."

Bowman swore comprehensively. "I suppose you're not pulling my leg," he grunted suspiciously. "I admit 1 wouldn't have believed it."

"True for all that. Both admitted the whole thing."

"Good for you I must say. But what have you done? No arrests?"

"Matter for the CC," French pointed out. "All the same I don't think it's as bad as it sounds. They both swear Selmer was trying to murder Pauline and she did it in self-defence. Of course one can't be absolutely sure at this stage, but personally I believe they're speaking the truth."

"Tell me."

French did so in detail. They discussed the matter further and Bowman eventually admitted that he believed French was right. "But I tell you," he went on, "all this raises another point. The inquest's at ten, so we've less than an hour to settle what we're going to tell the coroner."

"I intended to speak to you about that," French returned. "I suggest keeping this back and asking for an adjournment."

Bowman was not so sure. The inquest on Maurice had not been completed and he would dislike having another adjournment. The coroner, too, would probably object. "Just why do you advise it?" he asked.

"I don't think," French said bluntly, "we've got to the bottom of the thing yet."

Bowman looked his question and French went on. "When Mrs Selmer thought George had carried Maurice to the railway she was wrong. She didn't know about the prints. But he'd been up to something equally bad since he was ready to kill her to keep it secret. What was it?"

"You're right."

"I suggest we carry on a bit longer. There are some lines we haven't yet worked," and he told of the note about plasticine and cement signed "A R"

Bowman sat thinking for a moment, then he nodded. "Very well, French, as you say. I'll go and see the coroner and try to persuade him. He's quite a good chap and I don't expect there'll be any difficulty. But these fellows are fairly set on their dignity."

"Don't I know it?" French said with feeling.

Bowman's mission proved successful. The coroner, having been told the facts, agreed that further investigation would be desirable before his jury should reach their verdict. He also said that to obtain proof of the corpse's identity would be plenty for one sitting.

Before the hearing French took an opportunity to hint to Pauline and Rodney that unless they were asked the direct question they should not volunteer about Pauline having killed George in self-defence or Rodney's attempt to fake the evidence. "There will be an adjournment," he explained, "and the coroner may prefer to take those matters at the second sitting."

In French's view the proceedings were handled adroitly. The coroner began by telling the jury that they would have two duties to perform and that neither would be easy. First, they would have to say, if they could, whose was the body which had been found, and secondly, they would record their opinion, again if they could, as to how the deceased had met his death. "The body," he went on, "has been so disfigured by the fire that ocular identification is impossible, and the evidence of identity which will be laid before you may or may not be sufficient to convince you. That we shall now ascertain."

Upon this the coroner called Pauline. He was polite and gentle with her, expressing regret that his duty forced him to examine her. "Just answer what I ask you as shortly as possible," he advised, "and we shall get the ordeal over quickly."

He then began his questions, carefully avoiding giving her an opportunity of telling her story in her own words. Most of his questions she answered with "Yes" or "No", and he did not encourage elaboration. She had been alone in the Bungalow on the fatal evening until George arrived. He had done so about nine. She had noticed that he had taken a little drink. No, he was not drunk, but he was rather quarrelsome. She had therefore left him in the Bungalow and gone up to Cheddon House, believing that he would go to bed and sleep off his unpleasant mood. She had sat first with Sir Leigh and then with Brigadier Vale, and while doing so there had been a telephone message that the Bungalow was on fire. Major Vale had heard the news at the same time, and she and the two brothers had hurried down to find the Fire Brigade in charge. She had later been shown by Sergeant Dutton the point in the building at which the body had been found, and it was where her husband's bed had stood.

Sergeant Dutton then gave evidence that a body had been found at the spot which he had pointed out to the last witness, and that this body was that upon which the inquest was being held. He confirmed the coroner's remark as to the impossibility of ocular identification, but added that so far as was known, George Selmer had disappeared at the time of the conflagration.

This appeared to satisfy the coroner. He surprised the bulk of his audience by saying that he understood the police were still inquiring into the tragedy, and to give them time to complete their investigations he would adjourn the proceedings to that day fortnight.

"You fixed that well," French said to Bowman as they drove back to the station. "If we don't get something in a fortnight we can give up and drown ourselves."

"You're speaking for yourself, I presume," Bowman retorted. "Well, anything I can do?"

"Not at the moment, Super. I'm going back to the hotel to make up my notes."

The notes took time, but when they were finished French found he had still a couple of hours before lunch. This gave him an opportunity to consider the problem he had mentioned to Bowman: why George had tried to murder Pauline.

He sat down before the fire in the hotel lounge and lit his pipe and unhurriedly began to turn the facts over in his mind. It was obvious that George had seen danger in Pauline's suggestion that he had drugged her in order to leave the house unheard on the morning of Maurice's murder. To attempt such drastic means to silence her meant that the danger was vital, that nothing more nor less than his own life was at stake. But how? Or why? French did not see how George could have had anything to do with Maurice's murder. At the time of the knock out and injection he was in bed, and whoever had carried the body to the railway had very much smaller feet. George could not possibly have put on the shoes which had been worn.

It was an exasperating dilemma. George apparently had a vital connection with some crime at the time of the murder of Maurice. That murder was the only crime which had then been perpetrated. But the details of the affair showed that George could have had no connection with it. On the other hand, if George had no connection with it, why had he tried to kill his wife?

Finding no enlightenment from these uncompromising facts, French's thoughts turned to another point. George's illness! Was there not in the story a suggestion that it had been opportune? Could it be that George's action, whatever it was, required an illness at that particular time? In other words, had George brought it about?

French turned over the leaves of his notebook. Mrs Selmer had told him that on the day of the illness George had lunched with some business acquaintances in Bristol, and he and she had assumed he had then eaten something which had disagreed with him. French had seen an engagement book in George's study at the Bungalow and he wondered had it escaped the fire. He turned to Carter.

"Get out the car again, will you? Another run to the Bungalow."

The book was still there, having been protected from damage by the lid of the desk. On the day in question there was a note, "Simon: 1.00 p.m. Birley Arms." A telephone directory lay close by. From it French learned that there were a good many Simons in Bristol, but one immediately struck him as a possibility. It was Messrs Simon & Raynor, Agricultural Machinery Manufacturers, of 432B Chester Hill, Bristol. The same authority indicated that the Birley Arms was a hotel in Lanchester Street in the same area of the city.

Returning to the police station, French rang up the former address. Yes, Mr Simon was in the office. French's business was personal. A pause. Yes, this was Mr Simon speaking. Yes, he had certainly known the late Mr Selmer. His firm had supplied him with machinery. Lunched with him at the Birley Arms? That was right, he and his partner had done so on the date in question. Very well, if Mr French wished to see him, he would be in his office all the afternoon.

After lunch the two men drove along the winding road to Bristol. Mr Simon was a smiling pleasant-spoken man who said he would be glad to help them in any way in his power.

French thanked him. "I want to find out, Mr Simon, exactly what Mr Selmer had to eat at that lunch. He was ill after it and I want to trace the cause. Can you by any chance remember?"

Simon considered this, then shook his head. With the best will in the world he could not. It was several days ago.

"Were you alone with Mr Selmer?"

Simon brightened up. "No, Raynor was with us. He may remember." He spoke through a house telephone and in a moment another man entered the room. "My partner, Mr Raynor."

French explained his desire, but Raynor could do little better than his partner. He remembered that they had had soup, fish, sweets and coffee, but he was hanged if he could tell what particular brands of these comestibles were served.

"You'd much oblige me," French went on, "if you'd come round to the hotel with me. We'll see the waiter and anyone else who can help."

The partners seemed impressed with this demonstration of police efficiency. They went to the hotel and saw the manager, the head waiter, and the waiter who had served their table. The meal was reconstructed course by course, and this enabled French to learn with fair certainty what he had wanted to know: that all three men had had precisely the same food and drink.

But neither Simon nor Raynor, nor, so far as the manager knew, anyone else had been ill after the meal. It therefore looked as if George could not have had anything at the hotel to account for his attack. This was corroborated by another piece of information. In reply to further questions Simon said that after lunch he and Selmer had driven to a farm near Badminton to see some recently installed machinery. They had returned to his office for further particulars of the machines, and there had a cup of tea together. George had left for his home about half past four, then seeming in perfect health. Incidentally Simon had felt no ill effects from the tea. French remembered that George had arrived home shortly before half past five. He must therefore have gone direct.

In the face of all this evidence it seemed impossible to believe that George's attack was accidental. This appeared to be supported by another fact. George, though normally free from such minor ailments, had had a series of four attacks: that in question and three earlier of a similar but milder type. Could these, French now asked himself, have been experiments to ascertain the proper amount of dope to be taken? What this dope might have been he did not know, but he had seen arsenical weed killer in the Cheddon garden shed, and he had no doubt that a minute quantity of this would do the trick.

It looked then as if George had caused his illness and drugged his wife. Such actions were no sudden whim: they could only form part of some carefully thought-out plan. And what carefully thought-out plan of life or death importance had been carried out that night but the one? Somehow or other, French now felt convinced, George had had a part in Maurice's death.

If so, the real object of the illness at once became clear. It was not to enable Pauline to be doped: for that a drink at bedtime would no doubt have been sufficient. No, the illness unquestionably was an alibi. It was to prove George innocent of the assault on Maurice. It was also doubtless to suggest that he was at home all night, though for the small-hour period its evidence did not amount to proof.

If French were right so far, it surely meant that the murder had been carried out by two people, one knocking Maurice out and giving him the injection, the other carrying him to the railway. But what possible object could there be in such an arrangement?

A little thought showed that there might be a very real one. If two people were to benefit from a crime, it was unlikely that either would take the sole responsibility of carrying it out. Each would insist that the other should be as much involved as himself. So neither would bear the whole risk, and neither would be in a position to turn King's evidence against the other.

Were there two persons likely to benefit by such a crime? Rupert being out of it, the answer shrieked to heaven. Rodney and George! In the arrangement proposed by Rodney during the family meeting, the profits of the oil scheme were to be equally divided, which meant that if it went on, both Rodney and George would be rich.

But *had* Rodney and George entered into such a conspiracy? In Rodney's case there was nothing to suggest it, while in George's it seemed to be disproved by the footprints.

French struggled with the problem. In vain he tried all his tricks. He sat in luxurious ease before a hot fire, smoking and drinking innumerable cups of strong black coffee. Often he had found that physical ease gave a mental stimulus. But today no brilliant inspiration came to his aid.

Presently his thoughts wandered somewhat from the matter in hand. On George's desk he had noticed a copy of the Sherlock Holmes complete short stories, obviously quite new. He now thought whimsically, why should a man of George's type buy such a book?

It was some time since he had read the stories, but he remembered them, some vividly, others more hazily. That tale of the snake, what was it? *The Speckled Band*! That was a tale which couldn't be forgotten. And *The Redheaded League* and the horse that kicked its trainer to death. Yes, they were splendid tales! But what did George want them for?

French idly mused over the stories, recalling the fertility of Doyle's invention and his amazing resource. In those fifty or sixty stories there were fifty or sixty plots, all varied and all highly original and ingenious. French told himself he must refresh his own memories of the series.

Then suddenly an idea flashed into his mind. From so rich a collection could George have found a help with his plan? French could not recall anything that seemed promising, but he was at a dead end and he might as well go out to have a look over the book.

The long-suffering Carter having once again brought round the car, they drove out to the Bungalow. French experimented to see if the book would fall open at one place rather than another. A series of trials showed that it did. It appeared that George's interest had been in *The Adventure of the Priory School.*

It was one that French had forgotten, and as he read he lost himself in sheer enjoyment of the story. But it was not until he approached the end of the tale that he felt really gripped. As he reached a certain paragraph he sat rigid, thinking, wondering...

The tale hinged on the fitting of horses with special shoes designed to give the impressions of cows' hooves, as had been done by the marauding English barons in the Middle Ages.

Here was something to think about! Could George have taken the hint and added false soles to his shoes which would have made the Maurice prints?

French sat weighing the idea. If George had done such a thing it would account for all his puzzling actions. But was it possible? French did not know, but at first sight he thought it not unlikely. He turned to details. If George had accomplished it, how would he have set about it?

First, he would have obtained a pair of Maurice's shoes to work from. His method of getting them could be left aside for the moment: suppose he had them in his workshop. He would then have to copy them in some hard material. As it was unlikely that he could keep them for any time, he would have to make some record to work from. This might, French thought, take the form of a dimensioned drawing supplemented by photographs. George might then –

Suddenly French swore a deep oath. Plasticine and cement! Could he at last have reached the meaning of that strange sheet signed A R?

He went round to George's workshop and began a search. There in the corner was a bag of rapid-hardening cement, and among other old timber was a board on which cement had been mixed. On a shelf were two small rolls, one of fine wire mesh, the other of one-eighth-inch diameter wire. Snippets of both these had caught in the cracks of the sleeper floor.

There was more than wire in the cracks. He found also a number of putty-like scraps. But they were not putty. They were plasticine!

Full of satisfaction he returned to the hotel, and after dinner tackled his problem anew. He seemed to visualize a process in which plasticine moulds of the soles of Maurice's shoes had been lightly filled with a mixture of cement and fine sand, reinforced with a layer of mesh and lengths of the thicker wire. The tops of the castings would doubtless have been shaped to the soles of George's shoes. Some arrangement to fasten the blocks to the latter would have been necessary, and for the moment French did not see how this could have been done. He therefore bypassed the point for the time being.

The cement castings, he was sure, would work perfectly except for one point: their edges would crack or crumble if they came in contact with stones. They would make admirable impressions over soft sand or mud, but would not stand up to walking on the hard road.

He lit his pipe and continued musing over the problem. Where had the footprints been found? On soft patches only and on few of them at that. In the clump of shrubs at the silo, seven; between the silo and the railway, three; between the railway and the road, five; in Mrs Belcher's garden, nine: a total of twenty-four. There was no doubt that the cement would have stood up to use on soft ground twenty-four times.

Then French saw that the castings need not have been attached to George's shoes. Instead they could have been built up on pieces of board, projecting screws keying the cement. These could have been easily carried and when a print was required a casting could have been placed on the ground and pushed down by treading on the board. The soft places to be imprinted would have been selected beforehand, but for the actual operation a small torch would no doubt have been used. The casting would have been pulled forward when being lifted out, to give the impression of a moving step.

For a moment this seemed to French completely to meet his case. Then an ugly snag occurred to him and he began to wonder if he were off the track altogether.

George could not have carried Maurice to the crossing without leaving traces. With that extra weight his feet would have sunk deeply and in the dark he could not have avoided all soft places. But not a single such print was to be found.

This worried French for some time, then he thought he saw the solution. Since George could not have walked along the path without leaving traces and there were none, George had not walked along the path. What, then, could he have done?

The answer was obvious. He could have carried the body from the shrubs direct to the railway across the fields, over the wire paling on to the line, and then to the crossing along the hard path at the side of the track, called by railwaymen the offset. While this almost certainly had been done, unhappily by this time no traces of such a passage would remain.

French was pleased by his progress. He felt sure his reconstruction was correct. But he kept on reminding himself that so far it was only theory. Before it could be used it must be proven.

Continuing his musings, he saw that after George had completed his journey he would be up against a difficulty. He must get rid of the casts because if by some unlucky accident they should be found, he would be as good as hanged.

What would he do? Obviously he would break them up, but their wire reinforcement would prevent them from being completely destroyed.

Early next morning French and Carter were again on the job. For a couple of hours they went through sheds and lofts and disused corners where stones and rubbish accumulated, but fruitlessly. There were no old wells or other obvious hiding places, and at last French began to wonder if the castings had been buried. Accordingly the search was transferred to the areas outside the farmyard. Of these, the most likely was a small coppice at the side of the Bungalow which, for appearance sake, had been left in its wild state. Here the two men began, pushing their way between the thickly growing shrubs and tree trunks. Suddenly French stopped. At one place the leaves and dead bracken which covered the ground seemed somewhat irregularly spread. He moved one or two of the larger bundles and inspected the ground beneath. Then deep satisfaction once again filled his mind. On the ground were traces of clay.

"A spade, Carter, and we'll have this up."

While Carter was away French pulled back a lot of the loose decaying matter. At once he found what he was looking for. Sods were cut over a small square, and all around were fragments of clay.

"There, in you go," he pointed as Carter reappeared. A few moments did it. Not more than a foot below the surface they came on what looked at first sight like a collection of stones, but when French realized that they were really concrete and fastened in two lots with internal wires, he saw that he had his proof. A few moments and the blocks were roughly fitted together, making up the two casts.

French was thrilled. Here at last was certainty! And he had reached it in the most gratifying of ways: by the use of his own imagination. He had imagined what George might have done and where the proof was likely to be found. He had looked in that place and there it was! What more could anyone ask of a detective, even of a superintendent of the Yard?

But soon he saw that in spite of his good work, he was not very much further on. Proof of George's guilt would have been invaluable a little earlier. Now it was too late. George had made his escape. It was true that French now knew that George had an accomplice. But his identity still remained unknown.

At the same time the probability that it was Rodney was very much strengthened. Who else indeed could it have been?

Then another snag in his reconstruction struck French. George had copied in cement a pair of Maurice's shoes and

Maurice when he was killed had been wearing those shoes. But Maurice had many pairs of shoes. How could George have foreseen what particular pair Maurice would have put on, or rather, how could he have induced Maurice to wear those of which he had made copies?

Some further thought supplied the answer. Rodney again! If Rodney had taken Maurice's shoes to George to be copied, as seemed likely, he would certainly know which these were. What was to prevent him from slipping into Maurice's room after Maurice had gone out and looking what shoes were missing? If those which had been copied were gone, well; if not, could he not have taken the vital pair out with him and put them on Maurice after he had knocked him out, bringing back and leaving in Maurice's room those the man had walked out in?

Progress at last after heartbreaking delays and disappointments! Surely completion of the case was now a matter of only a short time. Eagerly French turned to the next item on his list of problems: where Rodney, if guilty, could have obtained the morphia and the needle for the injection.

But another hold-up seemed fated. He had scarcely settled again to work when he was called to the telephone. If he was not busy, Superintendent Bowman would be grateful if he would step over to the station as soon as he had finished lunch.

– 11 –

THE ELUSIVE ANDREW RADCLIFFE

Bowman looked up from his desk as French entered the room. "Bit of information just come in," he explained. "As you probably will be handling it, I thought you'd like to do so from the start." He turned to a constable. "Get that fellow Hope again."

"One of the old Bristol CID men," he resumed to French. "When he retired he set up a private inquiry agency in Bristol and has been wise enough to keep in with the Bristol force. They've helped each other quite a bit in one way or another. This chap was talking to a reporter who'd attended this morning's inquest, learned of the adjournment, and smelt a rat. He therefore rang up Bristol headquarters to say he had some confidential information for the officer in charge of the case. There, that'll be his call: John Hope. Will you speak?"

"Mr John Hope?" said French, explaining who he was. "I understand you have something to tell me?"

"Better to meet you, I think, sir. If you won't be in Bristol soon I can go to Radbury."

"It's Saturday afternoon, but still, will you be free in an hour's time?"

"Yes, sir. Quite at your service."

"Then I'll call at your office."

In less than an hour French and Carter were climbing the stairs of a tall building in a narrow street near the Bristol docks At the top he found a door bearing the legend "John Hope. Confidential Inquiry Agent." It led to a small room in which a pleasant-looking girl was typing. She smiled brightly when French gave his name.

"My father's in, sir," she said, opening an inner door. "Superintendent French, Daddy."

French was amused at this example of a family business. He nodded his thanks to the girl as he passed through. A tall clean-shaven man of a rather fine type came forward from behind a small desk. "This is an honour, sir," he declared, holding out his hand. "I've never before had a superintendent from the Yard in this room. Some tea, Judy. I may offer you a cup, gentlemen?"

"Thank you," said French, smiling. "Nothing we'd like better, except your information, provided it's useful."

"I can't form any opinion about its usefulness, sir, but apart from that you can have both it and the tea. A reporter told me about the inquest this morning, and it seemed to me if there was any question about the affair, I ought to come forward."

"I'm sure you're right."

"It wasn't altogether easy to decide, sir. I took someone's money to do a confidential job. Should it not remain confidential?"

"Not if it's concerned with a breach of the law, I should say. And if it's not, the information remains confidential."

"Thank you, sir: that's what I thought."

The conversation was interrupted by Judy's entrance with a tastefully arranged tray.

"My daughter, gentlemen," Hope explained. "She helps me here. I haven't enough work to keep her busy, so she's reading for a degree at the University between times. Two birds, one stone: which I've always thought a good principle."

They chatted for a moment, then the girl withdrew and Hope got down to business. "It was a strange affair: I've never known of anything quite the same." He picked up a paper. "It began with the receipt of this letter. Perhaps you would prefer to read it for yourself?"

It showed the old CID man in that he handed over not only the sheet, but the envelope as well. Both were typewritten, and the moment he glanced at them French experienced his thrill. The typescript was that of the three documents which had already figured in the case: the letter to Rodney about the indiscretion of the former housemaid, that which had taken Maurice out to his death, and the plasticine-cement note in George's safe.

The envelope was in no way remarkable except that it bore a Bath postmark dated 26th September. The letter was typed on the same sort of paper as the other three, and read:

77a Morley Street,
Bath,
26th September.

Mr John Hope.

SIR,
I should be glad to know if you would undertake a delicate and confidential job for me, and if so, your approximate terms?

It is concerned with the possibility of instituting divorce proceedings, and your part would be to obtain the evidence necessary, should such exist.

In the event of your undertaking the work I would send you with my full instructions a lump sum as a guarantee of my bona fides, as circumstances will prevent my visiting Bristol in the early future for an interview.

Yours faithfully,

ANDREW RADCLIFFE.

French controlled his excitement. It was impossible to doubt that Andrew Radcliffe was the "A R" of the letter in George's safe. Things were moving at last.

"An interesting letter," he commented. "You didn't by any chance test it for fingerprints?"

Hope looked somewhat crestfallen. "Well no, sir, I did not. You see, I didn't at that time suspect anything might be wrong. The letter was normal in every way except the writer refusing an interview, and it never occurred to me this was more than temporary. I mean, I supposed if he gave me the job we would meet to discuss it."

"And you didn't? But no, tell it in your own way."

"I wrote that I couldn't guarantee to take on the job without knowing more about it, but if I found no special difficulties when I received the details, I should be glad to do what I could, and I enclosed a slip giving my terms."

"Very politic."

"I've made it a rule, sir, not to take on anything unless I think there's a reasonable chance of success. Failures are a bad advertisement."

"I wish I could follow your example. Yes?"

"In reply to my letter I got this one," and Hope handed over another sheet. It was similar to the first: same kind of paper and typescript, and the same Bath address. It read:

28th September.

Further to my letter of 26th inst., and your reply of yesterday, I should be glad if you would undertake the work on the terms quoted.

The matter is as follows: Mr George Selmer, agent to Sir Leigh Vale, married and living at Cheddon Bungalow, Radbury, Somerset, is believed to be carrying on an intrigue with a woman, name unknown. Information is required as to whether or not this is the case. If it is, the following further items of information would be needed: 1. The identity of the woman. 2. Whether conduct has taken place which would enable Mrs Selmer to obtain a divorce; and 3. If so, what evidence of such conduct is available for use in court.

I regret that I am still unable to call on you. However, there is no real need for us to meet. As this commission involves nothing unusual under the circumstances, I am assuming from your letter that you will be able to deal with it, and enclose twenty-five pounds (£25 0s. 0d.) as a first instalment of payment and pledge of good faith.

I am not reminding a person of your experience and competence of the confidential nature of such a commission, but merely wish to add that I am acting for Mrs Selmer, who does not wish to be troubled personally with the matter. It is therefore part of the conditions of acceptance of the work that you undertake not to approach her.

Yours faithfully,

ANDREW RADCLIFFE.

"What did you make of that?" French asked.

"Well, I thought it was a bit strange. I know Morley Street in Bath, and it's a small back lane unlike where anyone acting in such a case would live. I supposed it was an accommodation address, but I didn't think that was my business. It was clear Andrew Radcliffe didn't want his identity known, even to me, not only because of his avoiding an interview, but also because the money came in untraceable Treasury notes. Of course that didn't necessarily mean anything was wrong. I supposed he had a reputation to keep up and didn't want it known that he was mixed up in a thing of the kind."

"His identity would have been safe with you."

"No doubt, but he might have thought it safer without me."

"You could have traced him."

"Of course, sir: I could have gone to the address. But I didn't see that I was called on to do that. The job seemed straightforward and the money was good. I thought if I took the money I ought to do what he wanted, and so I did."

"I don't think anyone could criticize that. What did you do?"

"Well, I didn't know a thing about the man or the place or anything, so I went down to Radbury and had a walk round and learned the lie of the land. I had a glass or two in some of the local pubs and picked up what I could. I learned that the wife of one of the farm hands worked for Mrs Selmer, and I managed to get drinking with her husband. A few glasses loosened his tongue and he said that the Selmers didn't get on well and it was generally believed there was another woman in the case. Mr Selmer used to drive away often on unknown business. It has always surprised me how much of everyone's private affairs is known in the country."

"True enough. But it isn't everyone who can get the information out of a countryman."

Hope grinned. "Practice, sir, and knack, as no one knows better than yourself. I went on to the farmyard and found Mr Selmer in his office. I'd brought some seed catalogues and pretended to be out for orders. I didn't get any." He grinned again.

"Poor salesman," French commented. "Oh well, you can't be everything. Go ahead: I'm interested."

"Well, I'd now seen Mr Selmer and also his car, which was standing outside his office. Then the tedious part of the job started. I went down each morning in my own car and waited in a lane where I could see his car if it left the farm. I did that for a week and followed him on five occasions when all was normal. But on the sixth I had a bit of luck."

"I've heard that everything comes to him who waits, but I've never believed it."

"It worked all right that time. Selmer drove into Bristol, parked in one of the big parks, and walked to a small good-class and expensive hotel, the Riverview. That was about half past twelve. I was afraid to enter in case he should recognize me, so I hung about outside. A long wait I had too, for it was nearly five when he came out. But I had my reward. There was a lady with him, and I could see by the way he attended her that he was pretty far gone."

"That was luck, though you certainly deserved it."

"I saw they were heading for the park, and hurried round by another street and got there first and was in my car before they turned up. The lady got into Selmer's, and when they started I followed. They drove out into the country and there the lady got out. I passed them and hid the car on a side road. The lady walked on and Selmer drove away. I followed the lady to a small house named Myrtle Cottage, where she obviously lived, as she let herself in with a key and didn't go out again for as long as I watched, I suppose a couple of hours."

"A fine piece of work."

"Thank you, sir: it was the only way I could think, of getting the information. It was easy to find out who the lady was: a Mrs Joicey, the young widow of an old doctor."

"Local again?"

"Yes, sir. I noticed telephone wires to the house, so I went into a nearby call-box and got the name of the exchange. It didn't take very long with the directory to go through the names in that exchange till I came to Myrtle Cottage. That gave me her name. At the local I asked if there was a Mrs Joicey of Myrtle Cottage in the district, as I understood she had a dachshund pup for sale and my wife wanted one. It was easy to pick up a good deal about her."

"If you have the practice and the knack."

Hope grinned. "Well, sir, to finish the tale. I went next day to the hotel and by means of some of Andrew Radcliffe's pound notes got all I wanted from a waiter. The two met there fairly regularly. They always had lunch and tea in a private room, and he could swear to it and would if wanted. I gathered Selmer's tips weren't big enough."

"Expensive job, taking a lady to lunch. You replied to Radcliffe, I suppose?"

"Yes, sir, I set out the facts in a report and sent it with the balance of my account to Bath. A couple of days later I got the balance and a note that the work had been satisfactory."

"I see. Very interesting all that."

"Then today from what the reporter told me about the inquest being adjourned, I imagined someone suspected Selmer'd been done in. I thought I'd better pass all this on."

French nodded. "Well, Hope, I think you've done extremely well. For your private information I may tell you that we know Mrs Selmer killed her husband, but she has put up the plea of self-defence. This information of yours may be invaluable. If it's used I'll try and get you a decent fee for it. But of course if it turns out not to be connected with the death the police will immediately forget it."

"Thank you, sir."

"Now if you'll give me a note of the letters you sent to Bath, I'll go and prospect at the address."

French felt his brain reel as Carter drove him on to Bath. Who was Andrew Radcliffe? Was he the person he said he was: someone acting for Pauline Selmer? Or was he the person one would naturally expect him to be: the husband of the lady whom George Selmer was meeting in the hotel? Scarcely the latter, French smiled grimly, if he was dead; but was he dead? Whoever he was, the "A R" plasticine note proved that he was in the thing up to the neck. Indeed even without the note this was clear. Why should a man whose only fear was that his wife was meeting George Selmer, have written the letter which brought Maurice to his death? Or had Andrew Radcliffe done so? It was a proper puzzle, but there was no doubt where the solution should be sought. Radcliffe must be found. As if to underline the conclusion, Carter at that moment turned into Morley Street.

77a proved to be very much what French had expected, a small stationer's and tobacconist's trading under the name of John Fowler. A bell sounded as French pushed open the door. The interior was dark and by no means clean, and there was a general atmosphere of disintegration and decay. The meagre stock was heaped on the shelves without any attempt at a display. John Fowler, when presently he shuffled in, completed the suggestion of a moribund business. He was old and stooped and short-sighted, and blinked uncertainly at French through thick spectacles.

"Good afternoon," said French. "Mr John Fowler?"

"That's me, sir," the old man admitted in a whining tone. "What can I do for you?"

"You can give me a little information," and French explained who he was.

Fowler seemed upset. "There's nothing wrong, I hope, sir?" he queried nervously.

"Not a thing so far as I know," French reassured him heartily. "I just want to know about one of your clients. You give an accommodation address, I understand?"

This did not seem to reassure Fowler. "Yes, sir, I do, but there's nothing wrong with that. It's all perfectly correct and straightforward."

"I don't doubt it, Mr Fowler, and I'm not interested in your part of it. What I want is information about your recent client, Mr Andrew Radcliffe."

French could see a struggle going on in the man's mind. He seemed to be meditating a denial of all knowledge of the matter, then obviously thought better of it. But he did attempt a half-hearted refusal. "You understand, sir, that all my business is confidential. That's what I'm paid for."

"Your business is confidential and the police are not interested in it as long as the law is not broken," French told him somewhat grimly, "but we have reason to suspect that Mr Radcliffe may be concerned in a murder. You cannot therefore afford to keep back information about him, and I'm sure as a good citizen you wouldn't wish to."

Fowler was clearly horrified. "A murder!" he repeated weakly. "Oh, that's dreadful! Dreadful! But I don't know anything about it."

"I don't suggest that you do. But because of it you'll see that you must answer my questions. Now tell me all you can about Mr Radcliffe."

He was frightened, was the old man, and came over at once with his story. French thought he was doing his best, but the recital was exasperatingly unhelpful. It appeared that seven weeks earlier a man had come into the shop and said he was moving about the country and wanted the accommodation of an address until he should find some place to live. He gave his name as Mr Andrew Radcliffe and paid the usual fees. Three letters had come for him and he had called for them. Fowler had not noted the dates, but his recollection agreed fairly well with those given by Hope.

When asked to describe Radcliffe, Fowler either could not or would not do so. The shop was dark and Radcliffe had stood with his back to what light there was. He was of medium height and slightish build, was dressed in a soft hat and waterproof, and had no distinguishing characteristics that Fowler had noticed. Except one: he spoke with a strong Scotch accent. French did all he could to get further information, but without success. He thought this was not Fowler's fault and that the man was doing his best. All the same, the description could apply to almost anyone and the accent might have been imitated.

Tired and somewhat dispirited, he and Carter drove back to Radbury. Bowman was just going home, but when he saw French he turned back into his room. "Well?" he asked. "Was Hope any use to you?"

French described his afternoon. Bowman was impressed and said he could understand French's exasperation. Then he went on: "You may have drawn a blank at Bath, but you've had a bit of luck here. The CC turned up unexpectedly a couple of hours ago. He wanted to know what you'd been doing so I repeated your story at second-hand. I can tell you it gave him a knock. George and Pauline Selmer and Rodney Vale all in the thing up to their necks. He twisted and grunted and didn't know what to say. Then he asked what your views were about an arrest. I told him you were inclined to postpone it. He leaped at that: said you were in charge and responsible and we ought to defer to your opinion. So nothing's to be done for the present."

"As a matter of fact," said French, "I really do think that's wise. I feel there's a lot more in the case than we've got yet, and we've more chance of getting it if we don't show our hand."

"That will be OK by him, as he always says, always adding, 'As the foul phrase has it'."

Somewhat shortly French said good night and returned to the hotel. Though the case was progressing, he had at the moment a grudge against fate. This was Saturday evening, and Saturday evening he always tried to spend with his wife. Had Hope not rung up, he would now doubtless have been as far on his way as Didcot or Reading. Carter also, he knew, wanted a day at home. It was just, he told himself, another example of the crooked way things happened.

There was plenty of work to be done on his notes, but French for once did not feel like work. He realized that staleness was threatening, and when that happened inclination miraculously became backed up by duty. He turned to Carter. "Any views for an evening off, Sergeant? What about the cinema here? Or would you rather go into Bristol?"

Carter would do anything his superior suggested, as was meet, but so far as he was concerned himself, he'd had enough of Bristol for one day. As a matter of fact, unless French wished otherwise, he'd be content enough where he was. There was a good fire and he'd found an interesting book, and anyhow it was a pouring night outside.

French was pleased with the suggestion. He also had an interesting book. He liked tales of the sea and he had dropped into his bag an early Humfrey Jordan which promised great things. They drew up the two easiest chairs, lit pipes, and while Carter moved in spirit through the gaming rooms of Monte Carlo, French threshed perilously across the Great Australian Bight in the teeth of a vicious sou'-easter.

Next morning was Sunday and the problem again arose, to work or not to work? But both men felt that since they couldn't get home, they might as well get on with the job. Carter accordingly brought out the car and they drove through Bristol and some seven or eight miles towards the north. Following the directions supplied by Hope, they stopped at a small property which bore on its gate the name Myrtle Cottage.

"Money, but not a great deal," said French, running his eye over the tiny garden, tastefully laid out in grass and shrubs with a few flowers here and there, all in reasonably good order. "Shrubs like those cost something and she doesn't find it necessary to grow fruit or vegetables."

French recognized Mrs Joicey from Hope's description, as she opened the door and stood looking at them in placid silence. She was a good-looking woman, tallish and fair and blue-eyed, with a creamy complexion which French thought owed a little to art. She seemed to possess an aura of calm which was in no wise ruffled when French proclaimed his calling, though some slight mystification showed in her expression. "Come in," she invited in a surprisingly deep voice, leading the way to a small pleasantly furnished sitting-room. She pointed to chairs and sat down restfully herself.

"I'm investigating the death of the late Mr George Selmer," French began abruptly, hoping to shake that calm poise. He did not exactly succeed, though a wary look flashed for a moment in her eyes.

"Mr George Selmer?" she repeated. "I saw in the paper that someone of the name had died, but I don't see why you should come to me about it."

French shook his bead. "I'm afraid that line won't help you, Mrs Joicey," he said gravely. "The police know about your friendship with Mr Selmer and of your meetings with him at the Riverview Hotel. To pretend ignorance will be, if I may say so, very foolish on your part."

"What unpleasant consequences could follow?" she asked surprisingly.

"The case I'm investigating is that of a murder," French returned with something less than his usual straightforwardness. "I don't need to tell you that any attempt to obstruct the official inquiry may be serious for you."

She looked at him coolly for some seconds as if considering her line of action. "A murder case?" she then repeated. "That may make a difference. But I didn't murder Mr Selmer, if that's what you imagine."

"I'm aware of that, madam," French declared dryly. "I'm also aware that you may be able to tell me a good deal about him and I shall be grateful if you will do so."

Again came the pause. "What do you want to know?" she asked.

A few questions confirmed all that Hope had discovered and in addition French learned that the affair had been going on for some six months. George had told her he was well off and was living apart from his wife by mutual consent. Mrs Joicey had last seen him three days before his death. She had thought him worried and abstracted for some little time, but to her inquiries he had always denied that there was anything wrong.

"Your perception was accurate," French told her, "for there was something very badly wrong. Now tell me, please, who besides Mr Selmer was interested in your conduct or way of life?"

She drew herself up, slightly. "I don't understand you."

"We have reason to suspect that someone was, you know," French persisted. "May I ask if you have close relatives who might be?"

"None, and I fail to see how it concerns you. If I had, it would have nothing to do with Mr Selmer."

French ignored this. "No legal requirements or conditions which might cause a solicitor to keep a fatherly eye on you?"

"Certainly not. Will you please explain yourself?"

"Yes, fully, but just one question first: Who is Mr Andrew Radcliffe?"

She stared. "I don't know," she asserted. "I never heard the name in my life."

French thought from her reaction that she was speaking the truth, but he could not be absolutely sure. "You don't know then that a Mr Andrew Radcliffe employed a private detective to investigate your and Mr Selmer's meetings?"

She was obviously astounded. French was certain her feeling was genuine. He did not believe that any actress could at short notice put up so convincing a display. She showed the nearest approach to emotion yet exhibited when she declared, "You have certainly surprised me, Superintendent! I don't know who could have done that. Or why." She paused, then went on slowly. "But wait a minute. What about Mrs Selmer? Though she and George were not living together there might be some financial consideration which would have interested her?"

French assured her that he had not overlooked the possibility, but that what he wanted at the moment was her own evidence. However, Mrs Joicey could tell no more, or so she said, and this time he accepted her word.

"We'll have a word with Mrs Selmer before lunch," he decided as they drove away. "Straight back to Cheddon House."

Pauline appeared surprised to see them. "I didn't know you worked on Sunday," she remarked.

"In an urgent case we have to," French smiled. "But I can assure you we'd both rather be at home."

They talked like this for a moment, then French went on: "I'm sorry, Mrs Selmer, that the time has come to discuss a rather painful subject. Did you know, madam, that your late husband was in the habit of spending a good deal of time with a certain lady in Bristol?"

She half turned away. "Oh," she exclaimed, "is it really necessary to bring that up?"

"I'm afraid I've no option. Then you knew of it?"

"Well, if I must," she said with obvious repugnance and she went on to recount what she had seen in the Bristol street.

"Tell me, did you employ a private detective to ascertain the facts?"

She looked insulted. "Of course not!" she answered indignantly. "How can you suggest such a thing?"

"Did you know the woman?"

"No."

"She was a Mrs Joicey, of Myrtle Cottage, Willesham. Does that convey anything to you?"

"No."

"Now, Mrs Selmer, who was Mr Andrew Radcliffe?"

Pauline declared she had never before heard the name and French, watching her closely, believed her.

"Did you know, madam, that Mr Radcliffe had employed a private detective to investigate the friendship?"

This was clearly a blow. French had no doubt at all that Pauline had known nothing of it.

"But who could have done such a thing?" she exclaimed a little wildly. "Who could have been interested?"

"Well, somebody was, and I hoped you could have suggested the person." She shook her head and he went on: "I suppose it couldn't by any chance have been one of the Vale brothers?"

French had suggested this from the consideration that the brothers were so far the only men in the case who fitted Fowler's description. Pauline's indignation left no doubt of her opinion of the idea. Seeing that he could get no more from Pauline, French went on to put similar questions to Rodney. He also was, French believed, genuinely amazed at the news. He declared he had never heard of Andrew Radcliffe and couldn't think of anyone who might have taken this name. He had not done so himself and was positive that neither had Maurice.

French was a good deal worried as they drove back to Radbury. This matter of Radcliffe was a vital clue because of the typescript of his letters, and now it seemed to be petering out. Obviously the matter could not be dropped, yet French did not know how to proceed with it. Then an idea occurred to him.

"Tell you what we'll do tomorrow," he said to Carter. "Get some help from the local men and go over all the hotels in Bath and Bristol to see what men visitors they had on the dates the letters were called for at that tobacconist's. If the dates clicked it might be a pointer."

In spite of adequate help from both forces, the job proved a heavy one. But at last it was done, and to French's keen disappointment no connection of any kind was established.

After dinner on the Monday evening French was the victim of a deep depression. He had worked on the case really hard. He had indeed learned a great deal. He had cleared up the mystery of George Selmer's death. But he had completely failed in the job for which he had been brought to Radbury: to bring the murderer of Maurice Vale to justice.

What was so tantalizing was that it ought to be easy. There weren't a great many people who could have done it. So far as he knew, he had met them all. Which of them was it?

His thoughts returned to Rodney. By the method of elimination must he not be guilty? He decided that once again he must make an all-out attempt to settle the question.

He remembered that he had been thinking through the entire case when he had been interrupted by Bowman's message about Hope. If he were to try to carry on from where he had left off, could it lead anywhere?

He turned once again to his notes. Yes, he had been about to consider where the murderer could have obtained the necessary hypodermic syringe and morphia, and how he could have disposed of them when the job was done. French had a suspicion, and it occurred to him that Dr Manning might dispel or confirm it. He therefore phoned the doctor and fixed up an immediate interview.

"It's an SOS for help, Doctor," he explained after apologizing for so late a call. "I'm up against it and if you can't help me I'm sunk."

He had well sized up the doctor and he could not have made a better beginning. It flattered Manning to be approached in such a way by a man of French's standing, and it gave him an opportunity to impart information and feel superior. He smiled and said he would be glad to do what he could.

"Thanks to you," French went on with the good work, "we know that someone, let us call him X, doped Maurice Vale on the night of his death. Now for that I assume X required a hypodermic syringe and some dope?"

"Naturally, Superintendent."

"Where could he have got them?"

"Ah," said Manning, "that's the sort of question I might ask you. I'm only a doctor."

"It's the sort of question you know more about than I," French grinned. "When our brains give out at the Yard we use other people's. Seriously, Doctor, I wish you'd help me here."

"But I don't think I can."

"Strictly between ourselves my question is, where could Brigadier Vale have got them?"

Manning looked distressed. "I'm sorry to hear that, Superintendent. Is that the conclusion you've come to?"

"No," said French, "I couldn't say that exactly. There are difficulties in the theory. But it's a possibility I have to keep in mind."

"I suppose that's natural. But I don't know where Rodney could have got them."

"I wondered about the nurse. Would she have the needful?"

Manning looked at him more keenly. "The nurse certainly had a syringe and liquid morphia," he admitted. "I gave her an unopened bottle myself. Under restrictions I allowed her to use it if Sir Leigh had a bad attack of pain."

"Ah," said French, "that's what I wanted to know. It's up to me now to find out if Rodney had access to it."

"He shouldn't have had. The nurse should have seen to that."

"Perhaps she did. I may be on the wrong track, but it's something to work on. Most grateful to you, Doctor."

Eagerness had once again taken the place of depression when next morning French returned to Cheddon House on what he hoped might prove another major advance in the case.

– 12 –

ITEMS SUCH AS GLOVES

Sir Leigh did not yet require a whole-time night nurse, and Miss M'Candless, being thus able to get reasonable sleep, did not go to bed in the daytime. When, therefore, about ten on that Tuesday morning French and Carter arrived, she was able to see them at once.

French had already met her on several occasions and he had formed a high opinion of her integrity and strength of character. He felt that if she knew anything which might help him, she would report it directly and without evasion. He therefore told her openly what was in his mind, continuing: "You see, Nurse, we know that a hypodermic and morphia were used that night on Mr Maurice. We don't know where the criminal got his, but we know you had both. We want you to estimate the chances of yours having been taken and replaced."

She did not instantly disclaim the possibility as so many in her place would have done, but sat silent, obviously thinking the matter over. This was the sort of thing French admired, and when at last she spoke he was the more ready to accept her opinion.

All the same her reaction was disappointing. "I don't see how anyone could have got mine, Mr French," she told him. "I had it away in my case, and it is in the drawer of my wardrobe. No one would have known it was there."

"Ah, but wouldn't they?" French returned. "With a disease like Sir Leigh's anyone could guess that you'd have morphia and the means of giving it."

"I wouldn't say that, Mr French. There's many a doctor wouldn't trust a nurse to use morphia without he himself was there."

"You may be right, but as a matter of fact in this case the doctor did trust you and you had the stuff. Now tell me, did anyone in the house know you were empowered to give it?"

"Only the family."

"You mean the Major, the Brigadier and Mr and Mrs Selmer?"

"I don't know about Mr Selmer, but Mrs Selmer and the brothers knew."

"Very well. Now I'm not accusing anyone, but speaking purely hypothetically, either Mrs Selmer or the brothers could have searched your room till they found it?"

"They wouldn't do that."

French laughed. "I told you I was speaking hypothetically. Is there any reason why they couldn't have found it?"

Again the nurse considered. "Well, no, I don't suppose there is," she admitted at last.

"Was either the drawer or the case locked?"

"No, I wouldn't think it necessary to do that."

"And you go out for walks at times?"

"Well naturally: I have to."

It looked to French as if at last he was getting somewhere, but he wished he could learn something more positive. "I need scarcely ask you, but did you notice if any of your things had been disturbed?"

She shook her head. She had noticed nothing.

French stood up. "Show me, please, the drawer and the case and the syringe and morphia."

She took him to her room. The drawer was one of a number uncovered by the opening of one of the large doors of the wardrobe. The case was of wood, fastened by a spring catch. She lifted the case out on to the table, opened it and was about to withdraw the hypodermic syringe and tiny bottle, when French stopped her. "Tell me, have you given Sir Leigh an injection recently?"

"Why no," she said. "It's a bit funny after all our talk, but I've never had to give him one. I've never even opened the bottle. Dr Manning told me to do it if I thought it necessary, but I never have."

"Have you handled either syringe or bottle lately?"

"Not since I came to the house. I had no occasion to."

French sent Carter for his bag and tested both objects for fingerprints. Both were perfectly clear. This was in a way suspicious, though by no means conclusive. In so long a period the nurse's prints might have dried off. On the other hand the glass might have been cleaned.

She watched him with interest, then, before he could comment, broke in: "They haven't been touched, Mr French. I can tell by the bottle: the level of the liquid. In such a small bottle a drop or two shows. Nothing's been taken out of it."

French had believed he was making progress and this was a blow. "Are you sure?" he asked, unwilling to relinquish his hopes.

"I'm certain sure," she replied uncompromisingly. "See," she pointed to the top of the bottle, "it was just up to that wee shoulder."

It seemed conclusive. He had been picturing Rodney slipping into the room while the nurse was out and filling and removing the syringe, and returning it at the first opportunity when its work was done. But now apparently he was wrong. A syringe without morphia would be no use to Rodney, and if no morphia had been taken, the question was settled. It was profoundly disappointing.

Suddenly a further possible inquiry occurred to him. He picked up the morphia. "I see this was got from Topham Munn's in Wigmore Street. I'm going to ask you to lend it to me. If you want morphia Dr Manning will no doubt give you more."

He pasted on a label and got her to sign it. Then, smiling, he recalled Hope's approval of using a single stone for two birds. He wanted Messrs Topham Munn to examine the bottle, but since he had missed his weekend visit he also wanted a night at home. It occurred to him that it would be safer to take this priceless bottle up himself, rather than risk its fate to strange hands. He thought also a bodyguard would be desirable, so, to Carter's immense satisfaction, they travelled together.

He had telephoned to Topham Munn to expect him, and shortly before closing time he walked into their shop. His message had made an impression and he was shown at once into the presence of Mr Topham, the senior partner.

"I want your help," he explained after greetings. "This bottle of morphia was sold by you and I am assured that it has never been opened. But certain evidence suggests that it has been tampered with. I wonder if you could have it analysed and settle the question?"

"We can easily do that, Superintendent. But may I ask what you suspect has been done?"

"I'd rather not answer that question, sir. If this case goes to court I don't want the defending barrister to say I suggested what was to be found."

Mr Topham nodded. "I see your point. Then I'll get our man to start on it. When do you want the result?"

French at once became apologetic. It was a murder case and the matter was really urgent. If at all possible he would like it before the nine-fifteen morning train from Paddington.

Mr Topham hummed and hawed. Really things were so difficult in the labour world that he hesitated to give such an order with so little notice. But steady a moment! If the Superintendent would wait, he would send for Mr King, the analyst. If asked nicely he would no doubt agree to work during the night.

This was done. King turned out to be a perfectly reasonable young man, and when the matter was explained to him he willingly undertook the work. He would have the result for French if he called about half past eight.

When next morning French glanced at the young man's report he felt a sudden glow rising within him. A large dose of the morphia had been withdrawn and the bottle filled up with an equal amount of water. Here was a step forward! Here was certainty! Here was proof that at last he was on the right track.

An hour later he sat in the 9.15 a.m. absently listening to the rhythm of the wheels and watching the green country stream past, while his thoughts busied themselves with this new development. There could no longer be any doubt of Rodney's guilt. No one but he could have taken the syringe. No one but he could have dealt with the shoes. He could have given Maurice the quietus, and no one but he could have wanted to. Everything worked in: motive, opportunity, connection with the crime. Surely his case was now complete?

Complete as to knowledge of what had happened? Yes! Complete as to an adequate case for court? No! He could prove motive and opportunity. But that old snag, connection with the crime? No, that had not yet been satisfactorily established. A good counsel – and Rodney would have the best – would make devastating capital out of that omission.

French felt that though he was just on to his solution, he had not actually reached it. A little more work, a few further inquiries, and the missing evidence would be his. It had never been his habit to hand over an incomplete case and he was not going to do it now.

But though as far as trouble and work were concerned he was willing for anything, when he came to consider how he could prove that Rodney had taken the morphia or had dealt with the shoes, or even that he had been out of the house during the early part of that fatal night, he found himself at a loss. And the time which had elapsed since the event would not make that proof easier.

Inexorably the journey continued. In due course they passed Didcot, Swindon, Chippenham and Bath. But it was not until they were slowing for Bristol that French suddenly thought he saw his way. Would the matter of Mrs Belcher and her gloves not give him what he wanted?

He had to admit that he had neglected this line of research. He had not forgotten it, but other inquiries had seemed more promising and he had taken them first. He had not indeed thought that the affair was very vital. Now he saw he had been wrong. It might give him that connection between Rodney and the crime, the lack of which was holding him up. Eager to start work on this last lap, French went to Radbury police station to tell Bowman about the morphia and think out his new line of attack.

A visit to Mrs Belcher was the obvious starting point, and after lunch he and Carter drove out. By good luck she was at home and alone in the house. French thought she was looking worn and tired. She glanced inquiringly from one to the other.

"Has something fresh turned up?" she asked anxiously. "I hoped the matter would have been settled before this."

"You couldn't have hoped it as much as I did, madam," French told her. "I agree that it has dragged out far too long."

"Oh," she returned, a trifle confused, "that sounds as if I had been criticizing, which of course I wasn't. But this has been a difficult period and I'd be glad if it was ended."

French guessed what she meant. "I hope," he said, "you've not come across any unpleasantness because of it?"

She grimaced. "It has been rather unhappy. People seem to think I was to blame for the whole thing. It's a little unfair when I did nothing."

"I feel sure, Mrs Belcher, your innocence will be established, probably at the adjourned inquest. I'm sorry that owing to being engaged on other parts of the case, I've been unable to concentrate on your connection with it. But I want to do so now. That's what I've called about and where I want your help."

She shrugged. "Naturally I'll do anything I can. But I've already told you all I know. However, if there's some other point you've only to ask."

"Thank you. I'd better tell you what we've done. We've established that the footprints to your house were faked, and if at the inquest you say no one called on you that night, you'll be believed."

"That's something at all events."

"The whole matter of the late Mr Maurice's visit here was an invention to account for his leaving Cheddon House that night. We've established also why he did leave it, and it was for quite another reason."

"I thought so, but I couldn't prove it."

"Well, we can. All that part of the case is finished. Now I want to deal with the question of the gloves. I presume you've been thinking about that?"

"I presume so too," she said wearily.

"Have you any ideas about it?"

She moved uneasily. "Well, no, it's still a complete puzzle. I can't imagine how the gloves got mixed up in the first instance, and particularly how they got into the drawer in my room."

"I have now no doubt the gloves were deliberately mixed and planted on you. I feel sure also that the object was to call attention to you, so that the faked footprints might be discovered before they disappeared."

"It's very comforting to hear you say so."

"It won't really be comforting till we can prove it. At present it's only an idea."

"I don't see that there's the slightest hope of proving it."

"We can but try. Now, Mrs Belcher, I shall want a much more detailed account of your association with Cheddon House. You had been sitting for some time to Mr Maurice?"

"Oh yes, for three or four years, on and off."

"So that you were perfectly familiar with the house?"

"With the studio and its approaches. I've been to tea in the sitting-rooms, but never through the whole house."

"I see. Suppose we take a day when you were acting as model. Will you describe exactly what you did?"

"Well, when I got to the studio, I – "

"Just a moment. I shall want more detail. When you left this house did you always lock it up?"

"Always. I was most careful about that."

"What about the windows?"

"I always went round them to see that they were shut."

"And you're satisfied no one could have got in?"

"Absolutely. Not without leaving traces, I mean."

"Unless they had a key?"

"Oh well, of course. But no one had a key."

"I think someone must have had. However, we'll come to that presently. Now when you went to Cheddon House, what keys had you with you?"

"My whole bunch."

"Let's see it."

She produced from her bag a small bunch and explained what each key opened. But that of the front door of the house was the only one which interested French. He handed the bunch back.

"No duplicates?"

"There's another house key in my desk."

"Is it there now?"

The key was in a locked drawer of the desk and appeared to have been undisturbed.

"Good," French approved. "Now we've got you on the way to Cheddon House with your keys in your bag. When you reached the house did you ring at the hall door or walk in?"

"Oh, I always rang."

"So that Lamson or one of the other servants always knew when you were there?"

"Yes, always. At first Lamson used to show me to the studio, but for a long time he has just asked me to go up."

"Very well. Did you take your outdoor things off in the hall or go up with them on?"

"I went up with them on. A little room had been partitioned off in the corner of the studio, and I changed there."

"You left your outdoor things and bag there, as well as making up for the character you were to assume?"

"Exactly."

"I see. What I've been trying to get at is that your bag couldn't have been searched except in that room?"

"That's quite correct."

"Now here's the question I've been leading up to. Who entered the dressing-room while your bag was there?"

She made a helpless gesture. "But that's just it. No one did."

French had been pleased with the interrogation so far, but now misgiving assailed him. "Surely," he said, "you're not right there? Someone must have."

"I'm quite positive."

"Strictly between ourselves, Mrs Belcher, I fancied the Brigadier had done it. Is that an impossibility?"

She stared, evidently astonished. "An absolute impossibility," she declared. "You see, there's no other door to that dressing-room, and while posing I couldn't fail to notice if anyone went in. In fact, I'd notice if anyone came into the studio. People did occasionally enter to talk to Mr Maurice, but positively no one went into the dressing-room."

"Think carefully, Mrs Belcher. Was there no one at all? Not even Mr Maurice himself?"

She thought for some time. "I do remember now," she admitted, "that once Susan went in. She spoke to Mr Maurice and to me, saying she had forgotten the dustette, the small vacuum cleaner, you know, when she was cleaning the room. She went in and got it. I saw her carrying it out."

"Was she there long?"

"No. She would probably have to roll up its flex, but no longer than that."

"When did that take place?"

"Oh, some time ago. Shortly after she came, I think."

"Did you ever suspect that anyone had been in this house during your absence?"

"Never."

French continued to ask questions, but without learning any further details. He was more impressed by Mrs Belcher than on his earlier visits. She seemed a woman of sterling character and he believed unquestioningly what she told him.

On the case as a whole he had learned little from the interrogation, but as they drove back to Radbury he grew more and more interested in one of her answers. Susan! If Mrs Belcher were correct, only Susan could have had access to her keys. Could Susan in the time during which she was supposed to have been winding up the flex, have taken an impression of the bungalow key?

Susan? A maid! How could a maid be interested in such matters? Then it occurred to French that if it would have been easy for Rodney to obtain the syringe and deal with the shoes, it would have been easier far for Susan to do so. He remembered also that she had entered the Cheddon household in a rather unusual way. An anonymous letter had led to the dismissal of her predecessor, and she had turned up just in the nick of time for engagement.

French recalled his theory about the letter. He had supposed that Rodney had been planning Maurice's murder, and having learned that Molly Crawford knew something which afterwards might lead her to the truth, had himself written it to enable him to get rid of her. But suppose it hadn't been that? Suppose the letter had been written to create a vacancy for Susan? This if true would clear Rodney and would postulate an unknown. French grew increasingly interested. He must look further into the activities and antecedents of Mrs Susan Stewart.

On reaching the police station he looked up his notes. Mrs Stewart had called at Cheddon House on the day after Molly Crawford had left, and stated that she had met Molly while waiting for a train and so had learned of the vacancy. She had admitted not having had previous experience of the work, but said that from running her own house she knew what had to be done. Owing to her husband's death she had found herself without sufficient means to carry on, hence her application. She had lived in Gloucester, in which city Lamson had been brought up, and she had captured his heart by mentioning several people whose names he knew. Her statements had been checked and found accurate by the local police.

French saw that her story, while it might be perfectly true, was of the kind which an impostor would naturally concoct. This proved nothing against her, though it made him more determined to sift the tale. He couldn't imagine her having any motive, but it was too early to consider that. First, was there any flaw in her statement?

In case she might be implicated he thought it better not to approach her in person, and next morning he and Carter drove to Gloucester to follow up the matter there. He had the address of Mrs Stewart's house, and he began by an inspection of it from the outside.

Though semi-detached, it was of a much better class than he had expected. It was in a good suburb and stood in its own tiny plot, well planted with shrubs and grass and looking tidy and well cared for. It was apparently empty: the windows were shut and no smoke came from the chimneys, but as he walked to the door he could see that it was furnished. Ringing and knocking producing no effect, he went next door. It was opened apparently by the mistress of the house, a woman obviously well-to-do and of some standing.

"I'm sorry for troubling you, madam," French said in his best style and raising his hat, "but I'm looking for Mrs Stewart next door. Do you know is she away from home?"

"I think she must be, as I haven't seen her for some time, nor have I seen milk being delivered. But I don't know her more than just to say good morning."

"It was about the house," French went on mendaciously. "I was told she was considering giving it up and I wondered," he smiled, "if there was any hope for me. Do you know is it her own house or is she a tenant?"

"I don't know, but we're tenants and I expect she's the same."

"Then I ought to apply for information to the agent. Perhaps, madam, you'd be kind enough to give me his name?"

"Long and Latimer of Queen Street."

Ten minutes later French was shown into Mr Latimer's private room. He had left Carter in the car, and as he had not called at the police station, decided to continue in his role of private citizen.

"I understand that you are agents for 47 Beechwood Road, at present occupied by Mrs Stewart?" he essayed after civilities.

Mr Latimer bent his head and said that was so.

"I heard in a roundabout way that Mrs Stewart was giving up the house, and I wondered if this was true, and if so, whether you have a waiting list or whether I should have a chance of getting it?"

Mr Latimer seemed interested. "It's news to me, sir," he said, "that Mrs Stewart is giving up. At all events, she hasn't told me."

French smiled. "I'm afraid that ends my happy dream. My informant said owing to the death of her husband, she could not carry on."

"If so, I think she would have discovered it before. Mr Stewart has been dead for nearly two years."

French made a gesture. "That settles it. I think long ago I met her husband: a chartered accountant, wasn't he?"

Mr Latimer looked at him sharply. "A chartered accountant? No, Mr Stewart was an auctioneer."

"Not the same man. Well, Mr Latimer, have you by any chance another house of a similar type?"

Latimer's dawning suspicions appeared to have been dispelled. There wasn't as much as a cellar vacant in the town, he assured French, but he would be glad to put French's name on his books and advise him if anything turned up. French said he would be grateful, "if," he added, "such a house should be within my means. That one in Beechwood Road is just the thing I want. About what would be its rent?"

"Eighty pounds a year."

"I could probably manage that. Well, Mr Latimer, I'll leave my name and address, and if you should hear of anything you can let me know."

A few more civilities and French was back in the car. He was increasingly interested. If Mrs Stewart was as hard up as she had indicated to Lamson, it was scarcely likely she could go on paying eighty pounds a year rent, as apparently she was doing. Again, if she had to go out to work as a housemaid, why should she keep on so large a house?

How could he get further information? He thought for a moment, then went to the reference department of the city library and looked up an old directory. There was the name: Howard S Stewart, of Stewart and Bailey, auctioneers. He then drove to the office of the firm.

"I've been abroad for several years," he told the pleasant-looking young man who came to attend to him, "and I'm now trying to establish the death of an old friend, a Mr Howard S Stewart. I can't tell whether your late partner was or was not my friend, and I should be grateful if you could let me have some information about him."

"You'd better see Mr Bailey, sir," said the young man as he showed French into the principal's office.

"Last time I saw Stewart was at his wedding," French declared mendaciously. "He married a tall, fair, rather good-looking woman."

"That's right. It was quite a romance. She was a nurse at the local hospital and he had an accident and she nursed him. And that was that. Pity it didn't turn out better."

"I heard there was some trouble," French said innocently, "but I'm afraid I've been out of touch all these years and I never learned details. Did they not get on?"

Bailey shrugged. "No business of mine of course. But she was supposed to be carrying on with another man. Matter of fact Stewart had instituted divorce proceedings when he was killed."

"Oh," said French, "I didn't know he was killed?"

"Yes. Motor accident. Distressing, the whole affair." The curve of French's interest had risen sharply during the interview. The divorce proceedings did not concern him, but the lady's earlier calling did. A qualified nurse taking a situation as housemaid? Was it likely? Further. Here was someone who knew how to use a hypodermic syringe. What if Mrs Stewart had not only borrowed the nurse's property, but used it?

If so, she and George Selmer must have been accomplices. How they might have come in contact French could not surmise, but if they had done so and had agreed to commit the crime, he could imagine how they had jointly carried it out.

Susan had left her vacuum cleaner in the studio dressing-room so that she could go for it while Mrs Belcher was posing. It would be a matter of a few moments only to open the lady's bag and take an impression of her house key. She would hand the impression to George, who would make or get made the key. With this Susan could enter Mrs Belcher's bungalow in order to plant evidence of Maurice's presence. Doubtless she had noticed that Maurice and Mrs Belcher had gloves of a somewhat similar appearance, and if she had found the lady's in her drawer, it might have given her the idea she used.

This matter decided, Susan had no doubt handed over a pair of Maurice's shoes to George, so that he could make his plasticine negatives. One or other would type the letter to take Maurice to the clump of shrubs. On the fateful day Susan would plant the gloves. That night, after Maurice had gone out, she would look what shoes he was wearing, and if they were not those which had been copied, she would take the latter out with her to the shrubbery. She would also take the syringe, which she had borrowed and loaded with morphia. At the shrubbery she would steal up behind Maurice and knock him out by a blow on the head. Having thus rendered him helpless, she would give him the injection, if necessary also changing his shoes. She would leave him lying hidden among the shrubs, go back to Cheddon House, return the syringe, and her work would be done. George would later come out, carry Maurice to the crossing, make the footprints, and hide the casts. Everything would then be in order for the coroner and police to conclude that Maurice had accidentally been killed while returning home after a night spent with Mrs Belcher.

That George had been the moving spirit in the affair was confirmed by the fact that the letter which had caused Rodney to dismiss Molly Crawford had referred to the oil. This matter was known only to members of the family, and obviously none but George could have written it.

And why? What might have been the motive of it all?

On this point French felt that there could be little doubt. The oil! If Maurice were out of the way the scheme would no longer be blocked and George would come in for a share of the enormous profits. No doubt Susan Stewart would get her rake-off, but even so, George would be a rich man.

French wondered if the idea had further been that Rodney would be suspected of the crime and executed? If so, George's share would be vastly increased. But whether or not, George would have had ample motive.

Here for the first time was a really comprehensive theory of the case and French was delighted with it. But though he was himself satisfied, his work was by no means finished. The guilt of George had been proved, but not that of Susan. Some further evidence must be obtained to ensure a verdict when the case went into court.

He set himself to consider just what Susan must have done about the gloves. Clearly four operations would have been necessary.

1. To take one of Maurice's gloves from the pocket of his overcoat, which hung in Cheddon House hall.

2. To carry the glove to the Bungalow and leave it in the drawer in Mrs Belcher's room.
3. To take from the drawer one of Mrs Belcher's gloves.
4. To put that glove of Mrs Belcher's into the pocket of Maurice's overcoat.

All absolutely simple, except that the exchanges must be made in as short a time as possible before the murder, to reduce the chance of Mrs Belcher discovering what was afoot.

It seemed to French that Susan would have visited the Bungalow when Mrs Belcher was posing, as only then could she know she would be undisturbed. This idea might be worth following up.

"We'll stop in Bristol for a spot of lunch," he told Carter, "then on to Mrs Belcher. I've something more to ask her."

A heavy witticism about French and Mrs Belcher hovered on Carter's tongue, but glancing at his superior's face, he thought better of it. They carried out their programme and shortly before three were back at the bungalow.

"A point I forgot yesterday," French apologized as Mrs Belcher opened the door. "It won't take a moment."

"Since you think you can clear me of suspicion, you're very welcome," she answered. "Do come in."

"I want you to go back to the day before the night on which Mr Maurice was killed," French continued when they were seated. "Did you pose for Mr Maurice on that day?"

"Yes, that afternoon. I remember thinking that I must have been one of the last to see him alive."

"Can you remember the exact hours?"

"We started about three and carried on till nearly six."

"I think I asked you this before, but please tell me again. Can you remember the last occasion before the tragedy when you looked in your drawer and found your gloves were there?"

"Yes, you did ask me and I told you. On the day before that. I wore my gloves going into Bristol. I put them in the drawer on returning home that evening, and didn't open the drawer again till I found Mr Maurice's."

"Now, Mrs Belcher, it's my belief that during the period between three and, say, five on that last afternoon, someone came to the house, entered with a key and planted the glove. Can you suggest anyone who might have seen that person?"

She shook her head. "Oh no, the house was empty."

"You haven't got my meaning. Might anyone passing or living near have seen the caller? Who might have passed? Who lives near?"

"Oh, I see. Well, yes, there is a chance. Try old Mrs Goodfellow. She's an invalid and lives opposite and her great pastime is watching the traffic. She might have noticed."

Mrs Goodfellow turned out to be a charming old lady. She was paralysed and unable to knit or turn over the pages of a book, and there was little she could do except sit in her window and look out on the passers-by. French marvelled to find her so placid and happy and without a trace of the bitterness which so often goes with such an affliction. She was obviously delighted at his call, no doubt a welcome break in her monotony, and she tried to spin out the visit by questions as to his work. Feeling sorry for her, French sat chatting for a few moments before getting to business.

He described an attempted house-breaking. "There's no doubt the place was entered," he told her. "Nothing valuable was taken, but still we should like to get hold of the people who did it," and he went on to ask his question.

He was out of luck. It happened that on the afternoon in question Mrs Goodfellow had a visitor there and was not looking out. She was sorry because almost certainly she would have noticed if a stranger had gone to the house.

"Does anyone pass about that hour?" he went on. "What about a postman?"

This was no better. There was an afternoon delivery, but it was earlier. No tradesmen, it seemed, delivered during the critical hours, and Mrs Goodfellow could not suggest anyone who might help.

"When did your friend arrive and depart?" French asked, feeling as if he were inquiring about a train.

"She came around half past three and left about five."

It was a chance and French dared not neglect it. "Your friend herself might have seen someone. Might I have her name and address?"

It was a Miss Soames from Radbury, and when French had chatted a little longer, he and Carter drove there. Miss Soames proved a tall rather fine-looking woman with a pleasant smile. She expressed interest in the theft at Mrs Belcher's and was surprised that it had not been investigated earlier.

"I was sent here in connection with the death of Mr Maurice Vale," French explained with truth, continuing less accurately: "This theft is a small matter and had to lie over while I was engaged with the other."

He thought from her manner she was going to ask him why a superintendent from Scotland Yard should have occupied himself with such a trifle, but instead she shrugged. "Police methods are not for the outsider to comprehend," she declared darkly. "What can I do for you?"

It seemed here again that French's luck was out. Miss Soames had seen no one approaching or leaving the bungalow. But when he put his second question he at last received an affirmative reply.

"Yes, the Radbury laundry man was delivering next door as I left Mrs Goodfellow's. I noticed him particularly because his van had stopped just in front of my car, and I had to back before I could get away."

Once again French dared not miss the chance. He went to the laundry office, saw the manager, and put his question. The manager called a clerk, rosters were looked up, and it was ascertained that Joe Cairns had been the van man in question.

"Fix up for the Superintendent to see him," directed the manager, washing his hands of further connection with the affair.

"I think he's in now," the clerk considered as they left the managerial sanctum. "Come in here and I'll see if I can find him."

Then at last French's perseverance was rewarded, and handsomely. Cairns remembered the afternoon as the one before the tragedy. Also he recalled the small car which had stopped just where he had wished to place his van. "Yes," he went on, "I saw someone coming out of Mrs Belcher's gate that afternoon. I was just across the road and I saw her clearly."

"What time was that, Cairns?"

"Just on to five, I reckon, but I couldn't be sure to a few minutes."

"Good enough. Did you recognize the woman?"

Cairns nodded. "Maid up at Cheddon House. That new one came a while back. Susan, they call her. I knew her because she'd sometimes taken the laundry from me."

Certainty again! This information didn't altogether clear up the case, for Mrs Stewart's motive had to be established, but it was a mighty step forward. At last the end of French's long road seemed to be coming in sight.

– 13 –

THE BILL IS PRESENTED

When French sat down to dinner the possibility never entered his mind that before three hours had passed he would have solved his problem and to all intents and purposes finished his case, still less that he would have done so by the exercise of his reason alone, and while sitting comfortably over the lounge fire. But the fact was that what he had just learned about Susan Stewart gave him all be needed to reach a solution, and the final test of the correctness of his theory was easily and quickly made.

During dinner his thoughts were occupied with the question of whether or not to advise the Chief Constable to arrest Susan immediately. So far as she herself was concerned he would have ample justification, and if only she and George had been involved in the crime there could be no reason for delay. But this was just the point about which he did not feel satisfied.

His careful search through George's effects had not produced the slightest evidence that George was acquainted with Susan before she entered service at Cheddon House. If George had been her principal in the affair, their meetings must have been frequent, and French found it hard to believe that had such taken place, no slightest trace should remain. Though he had not had the opportunity of a similar examination of Susan's belongings, nothing to indicate that she might have been interested in George had anywhere been found. All this suggested, though by no means proved, that someone else had figured in the case, someone who had known Susan intimately or into whose power she had fallen.

This view was strongly supported, if not indeed actually proved, by the employment of Hope to report on George's proceedings. A man had called for Radcliffe's letters, and as this was obviously not George himself, it must have been someone still unknown or unrecognized: someone who could bend Susan to his will, and probably George as well.

At this point French grew rigid with his cup halfway to his lips – they had reached the stage of coffee in the lounge. Had he in his musings stumbled on something of value: nothing more nor less than the explanation of the employment of Hope? Had the unknown obtained his information with the object of getting George under his thumb? The information would certainly have the required effect. Pauline was unhappily married and if supplied with evidence of George's infidelity, might well decide on a divorce. If she won her action, as she would, George would lose his inheritance: Sir Leigh's will was crystal clear about that. Again, if Maurice blocked the oil scheme, George would get nothing from that source either.

It was clear that strong pressure could have been put on George by anyone knowing these facts. If he would help to eliminate Maurice the Mrs Joicey evidence would be kept back and he would receive his inheritance as well in all probability as vast sums from the oil. If he refused he would lose both and his job in addition. He would then be thrown out on the world penniless and without references which might enable him to find other work. Wealth or ruin! It would have taken a stronger than George to resist.

It seemed certain, then, that there was an unknown for whom both George and Susan had been working. In this case it would be unwise to arrest Susan now. It would merely be a warning to the principal to take cover.

French slowly lit his pipe as he continued turning these ideas over in his mind. Though there had been occasional suggestions of his existence, no unknown had actually appeared in the case. French was not concerned with the quibble that if he had appeared he would not be unknown; he was grappling with a new conception which these considerations seemed to suggest. Could the murderer, the real essential murderer, have had no personal connection with the actual crime? Could George and Susan have been his dupes, and could he have forced them to carry out the deed for him, while himself remaining in the background? Between them they could have completed every single item of the plan. Suppose, to avoid ruin, they had agreed. Could this be that most rare of all crimes, a murder by proxy?

Excitement grew in French's mind as he turned to consider what must necessarily have been the qualifications of such a murderer. He must himself have had a powerful motive: in other words he must have known about the oil. He must be highly ingenious and resourceful and utterly devoid of moral scruples. He must have been intimately acquainted with the Cheddon House occupants and *ménage* and aware of that strange item in Sir Leigh's will regarding divorce. He must have been equally familiar with both George and Susan and their affairs. Doubtless also he would have been far from the scene of the crime at the time of its commission.

French felt stunned as the shock of this description struck him like a blow between the eyes. Why, he knew the man! Had known him from the beginning of the inquiry! There was only one person who fulfilled the requirements: but fulfil them he did. Rupert Vale! Rupert Vale, though actually in London when the crime was committed, could be as guilty of his brother's murder as if he had personally delivered the blow and laid the still-living man upon the rails!

French gave vent to a great sigh. Here at last was the end of the affair! A little squaring-up and it would be complete, another brilliant triumph to add to the long list of his successes. A wonderful record, his! In the depths of his own mind he recognized what he could not say to others.

Then, as always, the reaction set in. That he was correct in his conclusion French hadn't the slightest doubt, but could he prove it? Had he enough evidence against Rupert to convince a jury?

He doubted it. Once again he had motive and opportunity, but nothing actually connecting the man with the affair. The negative evidence that no one else could have done it would not secure a conviction. Some further work would be necessary.

For an hour and more he racked his brains over the problem, turning and twisting in his mind every scrap of evidence which might bear on the problem. He was in a fever. Again and again he felt the solution within his grasp and again and again it eluded him. He set his teeth and swore that he would not desist until he had attained his object.

Then a further idea occurred to him which once again set his pulses tingling. That mysterious letter which he had found in George's safe! He had been unable to understand why George had preserved it with such care. Now he wondered if he knew.

The document had been typed with the machine used for all the vital letters in the case and on it was a fingerprint. He had supposed that fingerprint to be accidental. But was he wrong? Could it have been placed there deliberately? Could it in fact have been intended as a safeguard for George? Now that French came to think of it, it seemed to him unlikely that George would have agreed to carry out such a crime unless his principal was equally involved. Would he not have required certainty that he could never be denounced or blackmailed, or that the principal could back out if there was trouble and leave him to carry the baby?

If this letter – and here was French's idea – bore Rupert's fingerprint, it would amply fulfil this purpose. It would definitely connect him with the machine upon which the incriminating letters had been typed. The "A R" would connect him with Andrew Radcliffe and the employment of Hope. The mention of plasticine and cement would show knowledge of the details of the murder. If George were arrested and Rupert did not come forward to take his share of responsibility, the document would confirm George's account of the crime. It would, in fact, give George real security so far as Rupert was concerned. On the other hand Rupert could have no hesitation in meeting George's condition, for George could not speak without giving himself away. In all probability Susan had received a similar instrument.

If French's reasoning were correct, his next step was obvious. He must get Rupert's fingerprints. If one of them tallied with that on the paper, in all essentials the case would be finished.

He decided to go out to Cheddon House in the morning and obtain the prints. Then it occurred to him that he might not have to wait so long. Rupert was a frequent visitor to the local on the main road not far from Cheddon House gate. Perhaps with luck…?

As he and Carter entered the private bar and ordered pints, he saw his luck was in. Rupert Vale was one of a group having a heated discussion on some football matter. He was in luck in another way also, for the landlord was behind the bar. An old policeman and desiring to stand well with the force, he would, French knew, do what he was asked. As French leant forward to pick up his pint he murmured, "A word in private, if you please, landlord." The landlord took no notice, but as he stretched over to pick up some empty glasses he grunted, "Back door in five minutes."

French presently felt in all his pockets, then murmured to Carter, ending with the louder phrase: "I'd better get it now while I remember. I'll not be five minutes." With a nod he went quickly out. At the back door the landlord drew him inside.

"A police job, Symonds," French explained. "I can't ask you to do it except as a favour."

"Glad to help you, sir," Symonds answered. "What is it?"

"I want Major Vale's prints. Can you polish a glass, let him have it, then keep the glass for me?"

"Surely, sir. I'll see to it."

French waited for five minutes more, then re-entered the bar, slapped his pocket and said to Carter: "Got it. It was where I'd left it." He sat down, they leisurely finished their drinks and then as leisurely went out.

Shortly afterwards French was comparing the prints on a certain glass with that on the letter from George's bank box. Then at last he knew he had reached the end of the road. The print on the letter was Rupert's.

Except for a few dotting of i's and crossing of t's this really did bring the case – and French's pleasant visit to Somerset – to a conclusion. From the local he drove to Bowman's house, and from there they rang up Major Harwood, fixing up a conference for the next morning. At this French made his report, with the result that a couple of hours later both Rupert and Susan were in the cells.

A search of Susan's belongings revealed the one essential item of the case which French had not learned: the hold that Rupert had over her. It turned out to be simplicity itself: she was his wife. He could not acknowledge her for the same reason that had been used to entrap George: the conditions about divorce in Sir Leigh's will.

When, after having cautioned them, French told the accused separately what was known of their activities, Rupert blustered and swore the fingerprinted document had been planted on him. But Susan was of less stern stuff. Realizing that French's evidence must lead to a conviction, she broke down and told the whole story, in the hope that this might weigh in her favour at the trial. The facts proved to be almost exactly as French had supposed, differing only in one or two minor details.

Rodney's story of the oil at his meeting had profoundly impressed Rupert, who knew something about oil from his wanderings in California. Perhaps better than the others he realized the enormous wealth which might accrue both to those who worked it and those who owned the ground utilized. He determined that at all costs the scheme must go on and that his interest in it must be substantial. At his meeting Rodney had made a generous offer to the family to join with him on equal terms, and Rupert's knowledge of his brother told him that if the offer were not accepted, Rodney would go on alone.

Then came Maurice's opposition, devastating because he had the power to enforce his veto. Knowing Maurice also, Rupert realized that nothing would induce him to change his mind. His stand would mean, not that the pastoral country would be saved from desecration, but merely that the profits would go to others. The Vales would have to move elsewhere and they would have little money to do it. At all costs, Rupert told himself again, such a disaster must be averted.

There was one way in which it could be done. To give him his due, Rupert for some time fought against the idea. Then he realized there was no alternative. It was Maurice's life or his own – and the family's – loss and ruin.

He saw clearly that if Maurice were murdered, he himself would be the immediate suspect. His motive would be crystal clear and his record and character would clinch the matter in people's minds. Where suspicion such as this was aroused, a police investigation would inevitably establish the truth. Therefore he must have no direct part in the affair. He must in fact be away from Cheddon when it took place.

Pondering over the problem, gradually a solution formed itself in his mind. First the tragedy must seem an accident. Second, in case this was seen through, the actual murderer must have either an adequate alibi or no apparent motive. Step by step Rupert decided on the knocking-out of Maurice and the laying of his body on the railway. To account for his brother's presence there he worked out the faking of the prints to Mrs Belcher's bungalow. The scheme at length was completed, except that he could think of no one to carry it out.

Then he decided that to give security to the actual perpetrator, a joint murder by two persons would be desirable. Each would carry out a separate part of the crime. One would have an absolutely unbreakable alibi – because genuine – for part of it. The other would have no apparent motive for or interest in the affair. Once Rupert had got so far, the end was in sight. He knew the two people to use.

The first was Susan, to continue to call her so, for her name really was Barbara, the other being merely adopted as more suitable for service at Cheddon. Rupert and Susan knew a great deal more about one another than was suspected. As a major in the war Rupert had been driven everywhere by Susan, and it was during that time they had fallen in love. When Susan was demobbed she found that she had grown completely out of touch with her husband – for she was already married – and she encouraged the secret visits of Rupert. Harold Stewart became aware of what was going on, and after some stormy scenes he decided to divorce Susan. Before proceedings were complete he was killed in a motoring accident. With immense discretion, for he knew all about the clause in his father's will, Rupert continued at intervals to meet Susan. But he would not marry her as she wanted him to do.

Matters were in this state when the question of Maurice's elimination arose. Rupert knew how fond Susan was of him and was thus emboldened to submit his idea to her. Susan at first was horrified, but moral scruples were not her strong suit, and as soon as she realized that the thing could be done safely and would bring immense profits, her objections faded. But, she grimly determined, of these profits she must have her share. Rupert, in fact, must marry her. If he did, she would do the job. If not, and if anything happened to Maurice, she would go to the police with her story.

She had him in a cleft stick, and he knew it. It was: marry her or give up the entire scheme. He did not long hesitate. As a matter of fact he wanted to marry her, and if she would agree to keep the union secret, not appearing as his wife till he had received his father's legacy, he would be game. Since she could do nothing else, she agreed, and the nefarious bargain was completed.

They carried out the arrangement immediately. Disguising themselves as much as possible, they stayed in Leeds for the necessary period and were married in a registry office. Directly afterwards Rupert wrote the first of the vital letters on an old machine which he had not used for a long time. That was the letter to Rodney saying that Molly Crawford was talking too much. As soon as Molly left, Rupert telephoned Susan, and she, playing her cards well with Lamson, was appointed to the job. It may be mentioned here that when Rupert had written all the required letters, he dropped the typewriter into the sea.

The other victim was George. Like Pauline, Rupert had seen George in Bristol driving a stranger in his car. He wondered if George had committed himself far enough to be frightened by the threat of a divorce, and engaged Hope to find out the facts. On learning of Mrs Joicey he delivered his ultimatum: wealth or ruin. George also fought the idea at first, but Rupert had the whip hand and eventually George gave way.

Rupert began by fixing the fateful night for that of the El Alamein reunion, which he himself proposed to attend, thus providing the necessary alibi. The others believed that by sticking closely to their plan they also would be safe. The scheme indeed worked exactly to schedule. Susan obtained the key of Mrs Belcher's house and during a preliminary search for some way of suggesting Maurice's presence, found the gloves. Consultation with Rupert produced the plan of mixing these with Maurice's. Rupert typed the letter which was to bring Maurice to his death, leaving it for George to post in Radbury, and himself going up to London.

On the night of the crime Susan slipped into the nurse's room and obtained and charged the hypodermic syringe. She watched Maurice let himself out of the side door, hurried to his room, found that he was wearing the required shoes, and followed him to the clump of bushes. Crouching down, she could see him dimly against the sky. She crept up behind him and hit him on the head with a heavy ruler which also she had brought. He fell stunned, and she quickly gave him the injection. Returning to Cheddon House, she found the nurse had retired to bed. She therefore took an early opportunity the following morning to replace the syringe and to fill the morphia bottle with water to its previous level.

George already had made the shoe castings. He had also experimented with minute doses of weed killer, till he knew how much to take for his purpose. When the time came he took a dose and was duly ill. He sent Pauline first for tea, and when she brought it, for biscuits. This enabled him to empty the sleeping draught, which he had previously abstracted, into her cup. When the time for his action came she was asleep.

At the destined hour George carried Maurice to the crossing and laid him on the rails so that any marks of Susan's blow or needle should be obliterated. He then made the faked prints, and buried the castings.

The case that French put up to the Public Prosecutor was overwhelming, and both the accused were found guilty. Rupert went to the scaffold and Susan to penal servitude for life. Fortunately for himself, before the trial Sir Leigh passed away and so was saved this dreadful blow. It was held that the poisoning of George was justifiable homicide and Pauline was acquitted on a charge of murder, though Rodney received a short sentence for his arson.

And what of the oil? Rodney, the only surviving male of the family, was so sickened by the whole ghastly series of tragedies that, when he came out of prison, he could no longer bear the thought of remaining in the district, and both his sister Anne and Pauline agreed with him. All in addition were unexpectedly well off from Sir Leigh's money. Rodney sold Cheddon, divided the proceeds with the two women, and burnt the correspondence about the oil. The three went abroad to start new lives in fresh surroundings.

And French? French's brow darkened as in his room he picked up the file of a juvenile delinquent.

Freeman Wills Crofts

The Box Office Murders

A girl employed in the box office of a London cinema falls into the power of a mysterious trio of crooks. A helpful solicitor sends her to Scotland Yard. There she tells Inspector French the story of the Purple Sickle. Her body is found floating in Southampton Water the next day. French discovers that similar murders have taken place. After gathering evidence he learns the trio's secret and runs them to ground.

The Hog's Back Mystery

The Hog's Back is a ridge in Surrey and the setting for the disappearance of several locals. A doctor vanishes, followed by a nurse with whom he was acquainted, then a third person. Inspector French deduces murder, but there are no bodies. Eventually he is able to prove his theory and show that a fourth murder has been committed.

'As pretty a piece of work as Inspector French has done…on the level of Mr Crofts' very best; which is saying something.'

E C Bentley in the *Daily Telegraph*

Freeman Wills Crofts

Inspector French's Greatest Case

We are here introduced for the first time to the famous Inspector French. A head clerk's corpse is discovered beside the empty safe of a Hatton Garden diamond merchant. There are many suspects and many false clues to be followed before French is able to solve the crime.

Man Overboard!

In the course of a ship's passage from Belfast to Liverpool a man disappears. His body is picked up by Irish fishermen. Although the coroner's verdict is suicide, murder is suspected. Inspector French co-operates with Superintendent Rainey and Sergeant M'Clung once more to determine the truth.

FREEMAN WILLS CROFTS

MYSTERY IN THE CHANNEL

The cross-channel steamer *Chichester* stops half way to France. A motionless yacht lies in her path. When a party clambers aboard they find a trail of blood and two dead men. Chief Constable Turnbill has to call on Inspector French for help in solving the mystery of the *Nymph*.

MYSTERY ON SOUTHAMPTON WATER

The Joymount Rapid Hardening Cement Manufacturing Company is in serious financial trouble. Two young company employees hatch a plot to break in to a rival works, Chayle on the Isle of Wight, to find out Chayle's secret for underselling them. But the scheme does not go according to plan. The death of the night watchman, theft and fire are the result. Inspector French is brought in to solve the mystery.

OTHER TITLES BY FREEMAN WILLS CROFTS AVAILABLE DIRECT FROM HOUSE OF STRATUS

Quantity		£	$(US)	$(CAN)	€
☐	THE 12.30 FROM CROYDON	6.99	11.50	15.99	11.50
☐	THE AFFAIR AT LITTLE WOKEHAM	6.99	11.50	15.99	11.50
☐	ANTIDOTE TO VENOM	6.99	11.50	15.99	11.50
☐	ANYTHING TO DECLARE?	6.99	11.50	15.99	11.50
☐	THE BOX OFFICE MURDERS	6.99	11.50	15.99	11.50
☐	THE CASK	6.99	11.50	15.99	11.50
☐	CRIME AT GUILDFORD	6.99	11.50	15.99	11.50
☐	DEATH OF A TRAIN	6.99	11.50	15.99	11.50
☐	DEATH ON THE WAY	6.99	11.50	15.99	11.50
☐	ENEMY UNSEEN	6.99	11.50	15.99	11.50
☐	THE END OF ANDREW HARRISON	6.99	11.50	15.99	11.50
☐	FATAL VENTURE	6.99	11.50	15.99	11.50
☐	FEAR COMES TO CHALFONT	6.99	11.50	15.99	11.50
☐	FOUND FLOATING	6.99	11.50	15.99	11.50
☐	GOLDEN ASHES	6.99	11.50	15.99	11.50
☐	THE GROOTE PARK MURDER	6.99	11.50	15.99	11.50
☐	THE HOG'S BACK MYSTERY	6.99	11.50	15.99	11.50
☐	INSPECTOR FRENCH AND THE CHEYNE MYSTERY	6.99	11.50	15.99	11.50

ALL HOUSE OF STRATUS BOOKS ARE AVAILABLE FROM GOOD BOOKSHOPS OR DIRECT FROM THE PUBLISHER:

Internet: **www.houseofstratus.com** including author interviews, reviews, features.

Email: **sales@houseofstratus.com** please quote author, title and credit card details.

OTHER TITLES BY FREEMAN WILLS CROFTS AVAILABLE DIRECT FROM HOUSE OF STRATUS

Quantity		£	$(US)	$(CAN)	€
☐	Inspector French and the Starvel Tragedy	6.99	11.50	15.99	11.50
☐	Inspector French's Greatest Case	6.99	11.50	15.99	11.50
☐	James Tarrant, Adventurer	6.99	11.50	15.99	11.50
☐	A Losing Game	6.99	11.50	15.99	11.50
☐	The Loss of the Jane Vosper	6.99	11.50	15.99	11.50
☐	Man Overboard!	6.99	11.50	15.99	11.50
☐	Many a Slip	6.99	11.50	15.99	11.50
☐	Mystery in the Channel	6.99	11.50	15.99	11.50
☐	Murderers Make Mistakes	6.99	11.50	15.99	11.50
☐	Mystery of the Sleeping Car Express	6.99	11.50	15.99	11.50
☐	Mystery on Southampton Water	6.99	11.50	15.99	11.50
☐	The Pit-Prop Syndicate	6.99	11.50	15.99	11.50
☐	The Ponson Case	6.99	11.50	15.99	11.50
☐	The Sea Mystery	6.99	11.50	15.99	11.50
☐	Silence for the Murderer	6.99	11.50	15.99	11.50
☐	Sir John Magill's Last Journey	6.99	11.50	15.99	11.50
☐	Sudden Death	6.99	11.50	15.99	11.50

ALL HOUSE OF STRATUS BOOKS ARE AVAILABLE FROM GOOD BOOKSHOPS OR DIRECT FROM THE PUBLISHER:

Hotline: UK ONLY: **0800 169 1780**, please quote author, title and credit card details.
INTERNATIONAL: **+44 (0) 20 7494 6400**, please quote author, title, and credit card details.

Send to: **House of Stratus**
24c Old Burlington Street
London
W1X 1RL
UK

Please allow following carriage costs per ORDER
(For goods up to free carriage limits shown)

	£(Sterling)	$(US)	$(CAN)	€(Euros)
UK	1.95	3.20	4.29	3.00
Europe	2.95	4.99	6.49	5.00
North America	2.95	4.99	6.49	5.00
Rest of World	2.95	5.99	7.75	6.00
Free carriage for goods value over:	50	75	100	75

PLEASE SEND CHEQUE, POSTAL ORDER (STERLING ONLY), EUROCHEQUE, OR INTERNATIONAL MONEY ORDER (PLEASE CIRCLE METHOD OF PAYMENT YOU WISH TO USE)
MAKE PAYABLE TO: STRATUS HOLDINGS plc

Order total including postage:______ Please tick currency you wish to use and add total amount of order:

☐ £ (Sterling) ☐ $ (US) ☐ $ (CAN) ☐ € (EUROS)

VISA, MASTERCARD, SWITCH, AMEX, SOLO, JCB:

☐☐☐☐☐☐☐☐☐☐☐☐☐☐☐☐☐☐☐☐

Issue number (Switch only):

☐☐☐

Start Date: ☐☐/☐☐

Expiry Date: ☐☐/☐☐

Signature: ____________________

NAME: ____________________

ADDRESS: ____________________

____

POSTCODE: __________

Please allow 28 days for delivery.

Prices subject to change without notice.
Please tick box if you do not wish to receive any additional information. ☐

House of Stratus publishes many other titles in this genre; please check our website (**www.houseofstratus.com**) for more details